Hearts Larry Broke

New Fiction from
the Burning Rock

Hearts Larry Broke

New Fiction from the Burning Rock

killick press
an imprint of Creative Publishers
St. John's, Newfoundland
2000

© 2000, Copyright belongs to the respective authors

The Canada Council for the Arts since 1957 | Le Conseil des Arts du Canada depuis 1957

We acknowledge the support of The Canada Council for the Arts for our publishing program.

We acknowledge the financial support of the Government of Canada through the Book Publishing Industry Development Program (BPIDP) for our publishing actvities.

All rights reserved. No part of this work covered by the copyrights hereon may be reproduced or used in any form or by any means — graphic, electronic or mechanical — without the prior written permission of the publisher. Any requests for photocopying, recording, taping or information storage and retrieval systems of any part of this book shall be directed in writing to the Canadian Reprography Collective, One Yonge Street, Suite 1900, Toronto, Ontario M5E 1E5.

∞ Printed on acid-free paper

Published by
KILLICK PRESS
an imprint of CREATIVE BOOK PUBLISHING
a division of 10366 Newfoundland Limited
a Robinson-Blackmore Printing & Publishing associated company
P.O. Box 8660, St. John's, Newfoundland A1B 3T7

FIRST EDITION
Typeset in 12 point Garamond

Printed in Canada by:
ROBINSON-BLACKMORE PRINTING & PUBLISHING

Canadian Cataloguing in Publication Data

Main entry under title:

    Hearts Larry broke

    ISBN 1-894294-15-7

1. Short stories. Canadian (English) — Newfoundland.*
2. Canadian fiction (English) — 20th century.*
   I. Burning rock Collective.   II. McGrath, Carmelita.

PS8329.5.N3H42   2000   C813'.01089718   C99-950263-8
PR9198.2.N4H42   2000

Contents

- vii   Foreword / *Carmelita McGrath*
- 1   Like Spontaneous Combustion / *Lisa Moore*
- 13   Contribution / *Claire Wilkshire*
- 21   Talking / *Jim Maunder*
- 29   Archibald the Arctic / *Michael Winter*
- 41   Rust / *Jim Maunder*
- 63   Love Bites & Little Spanks / *Ramona Dearing*
- 73   The Smell of Holiness / *Medina Stacey*
- 83   Family Business / *Beth Ryan*
- 95   Stan and Edward / *Mark Ferguson*
- 113   Monster Ovulation / *Michael Jordan Jones*
- 131   In the Tent with the Macaroons / *D.J. Eastwood*
- 147   Learning to Breathe / *Jim Quilty*
- 175   Visit / *Claire Wilkshire*
- 185   A Drowning / *Mark Ferguson*
- 189   Afterimage / *Lisa Moore*
- 197   Let's Shake Hands Like the French / *Michael Winter*
- 215   Contributors

Acknowledgements

The authors are grateful to the following publications, in which some of these stories appeared in earlier form:

The Fiddlehead
"Contribution"

The Ottawa Citizen
"Let's Shake Hands Like the French"

TickleAce
"A Drowning"
"Like Spontaneous Combustion"

Best Canadian Short Stories 1997 (Oberon)
"Love Bites & Little Spanks"

One Last Good Look (The Porcupine's Quill, 1999)
"Archibald the Arctic"
"Let's Shake Hands Like the French"

Some of the stories were written with the financial assistance of the Canada Council and the Newfoundland and Labrador Arts Council.

Many thanks to our excellent, diligent and patient editor, Carmelita McGrath, and to our gifted designer, Beth Oberholtzer.

Foreword and Onward

*O*nce, not too long ago, an unidentified burning object fell into the sea off the coast of Newfoundland. When no debris was found, it was assumed that the object was a meteorite or a piece of space junk. Some time later, fire fell from the sky and immolated a henhouse on Bell Island. U.S. government officials flown in to investigate concluded it was ball lightning, weird weather. In Riverhead, ball lightning broke through the doors of a church, coursed through and exited.

It is from such fiery phenomena that the writers in this book take their collective name. The name Burning Rock connotes the creative and destructive properties of flame and the infinite possibility of surprise. It also hints that this place so often called "the Rock" is on fire, with creative impulses as diverse as fiery phenomena. Any and all of these connotations make The Burning Rock an apt name for the writers whose work is represented here.

The Burning Rock grew out of a creative writing class taught in 1985-86 by Larry Mathews at Memorial University. A group of young writers had gathered, had clicked in some essential way, and had recognized the need to forge some means of gathering more formalized than the regular but casual contacts that typify a large writing community in a small city. What evolved was a workshop group meeting every two weeks, alternating between the writers' houses, sharing food and drink as well as new writing, criticism and a constellation of opinions, and forming close bonds.

With *Hearts Larry Broke*, The Burning Rock marks fourteen years of creative output and exchange of ideas. The group's first anthology, *extremities*, published by Killick Press in 1994, sold out. The book and ensuing new work generated two author tours, one across Canada following the book's publication, and another throughout Newfoundland in 1999. In the intervening years the group has grown, changed, seen the publication of Lisa Moore's *Degrees of Nakedness* (Mercury Press, 1995) and Michael Winter's *Creaking in their Skins* (Quarry Press, 1994) and *One Last Good Look* (The Porcupine's Quill, 1999), and the appearance of the work of several of the writers in some of Canada's most respected magazines and anthologies and on CBC radio.

The Burning Rock remains larger than this collection. Founding member Larry Mathews does not appear here. Jacqueline Howse, whose work appeared in *extremities*, moved to Ontario; Natasha Maude, also in *extremities*, has moved on, though less geographically. Mary Lewis has not published in either collection, though she remains a member of the group, and has recently achieved a triumph of awards for her film *When Ponds Freeze Over*. This collection welcomes new contributors: Ramona Dearing, a journalist and fiction writer, now pursuing graduate work in creative writing at UBC; Michael Jones, filmmaker (*The Adventures of Faustus Bidgood, Secret Nation*), cinematographer (*When Ponds Freeze Over*); Jim Maunder, sculptor, blacksmith, art teacher, filmmaker, writer; Beth Ryan, journalist, fiction writer and educator. And as well as art, there has been a bloom of children born to the group's members.

But perhaps you are expecting a sadder tale, a sadder book. After all, it's *Hearts Larry Broke*. Whose are these hearts and who is Larry? Hearts are at the essence of this book; hearts beating, pausing, stopping in mid-beat, re-activated, the life force going on and on. And Larry is not quite the Larry of Carol Shields' *Larry's Party*, not necessarily the Larry in your neighbourhood who leaves his old carpet on your sidewalk, nor even Larry Mathews, who had the gift to have that room, that course available that introduced new writers to each other. Perhaps he is the everyLarry. This book might have been called *Slow Burn, Hearts, Blue Tongues, Like Spontaneous Combustion, Short Longings* or any number of other things. *Hearts Larry Broke* emerged from a flurry of e-mail correspondence and snappy argument, in the true spirit of a collective of our time. As Michael Winter, editor of the first anthology, said in a rather definitive e-mail, "The Barenaked Ladies don't sing about barenaked ladies."

Fair enough. Too much demystification can be a bad thing. When ball lightning enters your house, it will exit, as long as you give it space to do so. But you won't be the same when it goes.

Carmelita McGrath, Editor

Lisa Moore

Like Spontaneous Combustion

On the shiny collar of her black tuxedo jacket, at a potluck after Shelly and Ted's wedding, Eleanor notices a ladybug. Orange shell, two black spots. She is wearing, under the jacket, a crimson dress. The skirt a pattern of diamonds, folded like origami, each diamond held by a red bead, so that if she were to attain grace, or spill her beer, or be overwhelmed with some fleeting infatuation—she shouldn't drink in the afternoon—she can see herself, twice, in Glenn Marshall's sunglasses, her black patent leather purse like a match head in the red flame of her skirt—if she were visited by a moment of love, the beads of the dress might drop to the grass like dew or blood and the diamonds unfold into butterflies. She grips the wet beer bottle. Too cold to be outside. The tulle under her skirt scratchy against her bare legs. She'll shave them before the reception.

A big wind lifts the umbrella out of the hole in the centre of the plastic table and it pirouettes for a few seconds across the lawn on its white metal spike. Glenn makes a swipe for it, arm raised, fist empty. A wet paper napkin flutters off the table and dips, like a dove shot out of the sky, a gash of lipstick on its breast. The ladybug still anchored. Charles Burton smiles, slaps his bready knees with his hands.

He says, It's cold enough to regret Bermuda shorts.

Eleanor closes her eyes. The afternoon sways, the lawn, the voices. Once at the Ship Inn, Glenn Marshall put his hand on the small of her back. She'd been dancing in a black mini-dress and the cotton was damp.

He'd said, What are you doing?

Getting a beer. What are you doing?

Getting a beer. It's dangerous, talking to you.

Dangerous?

You have beautiful legs.

That was last summer. Just that, his hand on her back, the cotton damp with sweat.

She had screwed a fuse into a panel in the basement before the wedding and felt, through her fingertips, a throb of electricity. The current that powers the whole island. Dangerous.

Charles Burton comes back out with a tray of shrimp and melon, toothpicks with cellophane bunched at the tips. She crushes down her stiff skirt with both hands, fingers spread, and Glenn nods at her before he lifts his brandy snifter. She can see Walter in the sunroom window, listening to a woman with a blonde ponytail. The woman on tiptoe, he bends his ear to her. Eleanor sees him yank his tie. Then a moving cloud makes the window darken and she can't see him.

What's Walter doing? she asks Charles.

Walter is having a good time. Believe me.

She can feel the earth turning. The heels of her sandals driven into mud beneath the wet grass. She'd made a rice salad with sesame oil, red peppers. What else costs as much as a red pepper? A ball of Angora wool. Last night the taxi driver said, See that moon, that's weather. I had a wife once who could make a meal out of nothing. You had your moose, you had your garden. I got a different wife now, different altogether.

She had been napping yesterday and the phone rang beside the bed.

Walter said, I want you to greet me at the door wearing nothing but a martini.

Walter?

Yes.

I don't even know what a martini is.

It evaporates on the tongue.

It's too cold for that here.

Will you do it?

Yes.

You will?

Yes.

She got out of bed and wandered into the kitchen. Stood with the fridge door open, and fished a green olive from the narrow neck of the bottle. Held it between her teeth, the brine running down her fingers.

Just before they left for the potluck Eleanor had tried to knot his tie. She feels like her hands are changing places.

She says, How did you miss learning this?

He turns his head to look in the mirror. His face tanned from Florida, a conference. He had called her from there, leaning over a balcony.

He said, I'm looking at the ocean and there are people making love in the water. She'd heard the ocean through the phone and she swirled her fingers through the bowl of popcorn on her lap, pressing the chrome bowl against her crotch, licking the salt and butter from her fingers.

Won't they be dragged out to sea?

It's shallow for miles. You can go out forever and still put your feet down.

He cranes his neck to see the tie.

How do I look? He looks down the length of himself.

She tilts her head to study him and they stand like that until the cab horn jolts them.

Charles Burton was once in a helicopter, sighting the neck of a galloping moose with a tranquillizing rifle and they came near a cliff and whatever happened with the wind, the helicopter dropped for ten seconds. He told the story buttering a roll. Turning the knife over and over to clean both sides in the bread. He said in accidents like this the blades keep turning, driving down like a corkscrew, decapitating passengers.

Eleanor started it, making everyone tell the moment they had come closest to death. She told about the Nepalese tour bus, the front wheels over the cliff edge, the TV bolted to the ceiling still blaring some Indian musical with a harem of dancers poised on three tiers of a fountain, all sawing on miniature violins. When the second wheel dropped, the fountain hung sideways. She had seen, through the window at her shoulder, fire licking the steel.

Glenn Marshall leaned back and rested his arm over her chair.

The most famous person they'd ever met, the most romantic moment ever experienced, the most embarrassing. The worst fear. She told about her mother trapped in the living room with a weasel or mink. Most erotic moment without touching. These were the categories. The cork in the wine bottle rolling under Glenn Marshall's palm. What was his most erotic moment without touching. She can only think of the galloping moose. Walter said Eleanor had sent him roses in the middle of a rainstorm—someone announced it over the intercom at the bookstore. He was in the backroom tearing off the covers of old Harlequin Romances.

The woman with the ponytail sitting beside Walter, in a gold lamé halter top, said she had met Mick Jagger in Germany, rode in his limousine after a concert. Fans tearing open their blouses and squashing their breasts against the tinted windows of the car as they pulled out of the garage.

I put my hand on his crotch, he was wearing black leather pants, and the sun through the window made the leather hot. I couldn't help myself.

Eleanor said, That's not without touching. It's supposed to be an erotic moment without touching.

A man with a white beard says, I'm afraid of love. They are drunk enough to ponder this soberly.

She opens her eyes, and pulls the heel of her sandal slowly out of the mud.

What do you think love is Glenn?

He does not move. She can see the house behind her in his sunglasses. The sunroom window. She sees a white streak that might be Walter's shirt. She hasn't seen him in the garden.

Weasels don't come in white, he says.

Well, this one did. Like spilled milk.

I don't believe it, he says.

But you buy Mick and the squashed breasts?

She has an urge to tell him she remembers him touching her back at the Ship. Does desire have physical properties, like weather? Does it pitch on one thing, and then another? Can it spontaneously combust?

Glenn?

It occurs to her he is asleep behind his sunglasses. The children are running at the edge of the lake, her daughter, Sadie, in the middle. Holding hands, skirts whipping.

Glenn says, Love is an arduous journey. Like from this chair to that bathtub full of ice and beer.

She says, Last summer Sadie wanted a ladybug, but they only appear if you aren't thinking about them, you can't will them.

Glenn rises from his chair and the snifter of brandy smashes. She sees it fall, hot amber coming up to the mouth of the glass like a jellyfish.

You fix on someone, he says, you fix on them and that's it.

Lorianne, the groom's sister, unlatches the garden gate. Her pink scarf catches on a nail.

She says, The groom is at the bottom of Prescott Street directing traffic with two salad spoons, and now my scarf is ruined.

The wedding happened at Bannerman Park. The sun got hot for five minutes on their backs. The bride slitting her eyes against the wind. A few brave children showed up for the afternoon swim. The diving board reverberating, the smacks of their bodies against the water. Ted holding Shelly's fingers. He cried, unabashed.

There's a gentleness in Ted. Someone had given him a kitten for a wedding present. Sitting with Eleanor on her doorstep early that morning, while his shirt was being ironed. Ted opened his tuxedo jacket and he was wearing nothing underneath. He lifted out a new kitten.

She said, You've got a nice day for it.

He put the kitten in her hand. The fine pricks of fright, its pale claws.

He took it back, and cradled it in the rust lining of his jacket. It felt like a long time ago.

And she married him, Eleanor says out loud to Glenn. He bends and picks the snifter from the grass by the stem, the shards of glass like tulip petals, and walks off stiffly, toward the house.

She calls over her shoulder, You can't will love.

Glenn says, You can will anything.

Eleanor and Walter take Sadie home in a taxi before the reception. Apple air freshener. She meets the eyes of the driver in the rearview. It is the same driver. The one with the different wife altogether. She grabs her lapel.

Sadie look! But the ladybug is gone.

Eleanor's mother, Julia, comes to pick up Sadie before the reception. She's babysitting so Walter and Eleanor can have the night together.

Yes you do, you need it, she says.

Sadie in white eyelet cotton and a beige fisherman knit cardigan. Happy to go with her grandmother.

Carla, then, Julia says, starting in the middle of the story, Did you hear what Carla has done to herself? Shaved her head.

Eleanor's youngest sister, Carla.

Why would she do a thing like that? Come on, Sadie, let's go. Who will hire her now, Eleanor?

Eleanor feels the flush of wine from the potluck, sits down in the middle of the staircase, her head resting on a spindle. She closes her eyes and sees the lake of the early afternoon like an electrical board short-circuiting, sparks crackling, children with their hands linked, Sadie in the middle, running at the edge. She is overwhelmed with love for Sadie. Why can't she stay here with her? Why can't she and Sadie curl up in bed and sleep and forget the reception? Dusk, it's almost evening, and they could have ordered fish and chips. She'd do anything to be with Sadie, give up anything. Then Walter comes from the kitchen with a mug and spoon.

Lots of people shave their heads, he says.

He puts a mound of ice cream in his mouth, leaning against the wall, and pulls the spoon out of his mouth slowly, the tip resting on his bottom lip. The mound of ice cream like a fossil of the roof of his mouth, a soft steam. He sees Eleanor looking at his mouth and he raises an eyebrow. Immediately, she wants to be with him, get drunk with him, dance, she is grateful that her mother has come for Sadie. That her mother takes care of them.

Julia says, Carla had her back to me at the kitchen counter and I asked her that, who will hire you now?

Sadie tugging her arm, Come on Grandma, let's go.

She was getting a piece of toast and she had the butter. A block of butter in gold foil and in a rage she squeezed it through her fist. The whole block of butter through her fist.

Eleanor remembers a dream last night about bars of gold. A man put bricks of gold in her knapsack. She was rich. The corners digging between her shoulder blades. As if she were painfully growing wings. But the weight became lighter, and a warm grease poured to the small of her back. Had they melted?

She is confused for a moment at the coincidence, wondering then, if that had been what she dreamed. Or did she just think she had dreamt it because her mother said butter. Carla squeezed a brick of butter through her fist. There had been gold and loss in the dream. She was sure of that, gold and loss. And imminence. And something erotic, the oil streaming down her back. But was there butter?

It'll grow back, she says.

It'll grow back, yes. But she's in a fine state now. A bald woman. Come on Sadie, Julia says.

Was that the groom I saw directing traffic with two soup ladles? They got a picture of it. Someone did. A rose in his lapel. He'll be nice by midnight. Say good-bye to your mother, Sadie. Kiss your mother good-bye.

Sadie throws her arms around Eleanor's neck, their foreheads gently knock, they look straight into each other's eyes.

Sadie whispers, I'm going to have chocolate.

Walter squeezes past them on the stairs. Eleanor sits and listens to her mother's car doors. She listens to the car pull away.

In the bathroom, she and Walter stand side by side brushing their teeth. He pauses, his mouth foaming, the toothbrush still.

What were you and Glenn Marshall saying?

He gets in the shower. After a moment of looking at herself in the mirror, Eleanor undresses and gets in with him. The water hits his shoulders hard, like a bolt of tweed unfurling. She lets her wrists rest on his shoulder bones. Then she kisses his chest, down his belly, until she is on her knees. The water slides down his ribs like a garment. She makes seams with her tongue. She puts her hand on his chest and the water flows down her arm to the elbow, like an evening glove.

She says, Will I shave my legs?

Walter draws her up, takes her breast in his mouth.

At four-thirty in the morning everyone forms a circle around the bride and groom on the beer-soaked dance floor. They hold hands and sway violently, some of them fall over and the other side of the circle drags them up from their knees. Then those on that side, because of the exertion, topple and must be hauled back on their feet. Red stage lights splash over them, up the walls, across the ceiling, the floor. The bride and groom hug the guests, making their way around the circle.

The bride holds Eleanor's head in her hands tightly, she presses her cheek against Eleanor's cheek, and the bride's face is wet and hot with tears. She draws back and the red light falls over her, splinters of purple searing from the sequins in her veil, on the bodice of her dress. I love you Eleanor, she says, I love you. And I love your husband too. And I love my husband. I love everybody's husband. And their wives.

She lets go of Eleanor's face and falls into the arms of the man next to Eleanor. Ted grabs Eleanor and holds her. He has a beer in each hand and the bottles chink behind her back.

Eleanor tugs Walter's shirt sleeve.

Come home with me?

Not yet, he yells.

She is lying in bed waiting for him. It's 7:32. She lies still. There is a fear rushing around in her body. She remembers her mother calling a few years ago about the weasel. She was standing on the kitchen counter while a white weasel or mink, something that rippled like a stream of milk, was rushing under the furniture, hissing. What should she do?

Eleanor could see her, a tall woman, having to bend her neck so her head wouldn't hit the ceiling. They had both been terrified, both gripping the telephone receivers. Eleanor can feel that mink fear rippling through her body. She fell in love the first night she slept with Walter and after that she fixed on him.

A body slams against a wall and falls onto the opposite wall in the porch. It's either Walter or the three Norwegian sailors who live upstairs. The angry saints with their halos of white hair and steady brawling.

Walter lurches to the bannister, wraps his arms around it as if it were the mast of a capsizing ship.

I went to Signal Hill in a Cadillac.

Eleanor is standing at the top of the stairs.

We stopped at the Fountain Spray to buy candy necklaces and we had a giant bottle of wine. I bit the necklaces off all the women's necks. He burps.

Glenn Marshall's neck too. Spectacular Sam was there. That guy who dances on broken glass. Do you remember that guy?

He lunges past her and she follows him to the bedroom.

He says, Spectacular Sam poured cognac over broken beer bottles on the parking lot of Signal Hill. Lots of smashed glass. He lit it, fell into a trance and danced on it with his bare feet. Then he knelt and scooped the glass up in his hands and splashed his face with it, and drops of blood came up all over his face. You know, there was the sun too, coming up.

Walter struggles for a long moment with the buttons on his shirt, tipping slowly on his heels like a punching clown in a breeze. He sighs and rips the shirt open. Buttons hit the wall above the lamp. He falls onto the bed.

   She gets up to turn off the light, but he grabs her arm. Stay here, he says, stay here.

Claire Wilkshire

Contribution

I toss a bag of fat yellow sprouts into the shopping cart, and he picks it up and turns it around.

"What's this?" he asks.

"Bean sprouts." He stares at the label.

"Will you look at that." He passes it to me, and I read Produced by Liu, 12 Fleming St., St. John's. "It must be those people round the corner, the ones in the blue house." He's looking over at all the other little bags.

"Yup." I push forward into the Kleenex and paper towels aisle. "What kind of Kleenex do you want?"

"Mansize, you know I get Mansize—it must be them, mustn't it? No one else it could be." So I admit that in that case it's probably them. "Just think of it."

I say "Yup" again and start crossing things off the list. At the checkout I'm reading about the white Fiat in the tunnel and instead of just standing there like a normal person he starts tapping the paper.

"You could do that"—tapataptap—"start up your own business, supply all the major supermarkets, it's a golden opportunity." I tell him I wouldn't have a clue how to do that, and in any case it doesn't make a lot of sense to start up a bean sprout business when there's one already in place a few doors down. Also I could get offered a job any day now. "Not sprouts.

Something *like* sprouts. Make a vital contribution to the—" and I can see he is ready to continue in this vein, but thankfully it's time to start piling our stuff onto the moving counter and I assume that's the end of that.

I don't know squat about business. A fact he is fully aware of. Or what kind to start up. It's not like you can just haul into the shower one morning, flip up the cap on the shampoo, and think: I do believe I'll start up my own business. You need to know something about it. I could get a job soon. I've applied for everything. Anytime now there will be payback on one of those resumes, that's what I keep saying to myself.

That evening we're watching them do mouth-to-snout resuscitation on a dog on Rescue 911 and he's getting antsy, turning the sound up and down, not paying attention to the story. I figure he's getting up to go to the bathroom but he comes back with two umbrellas and a raincoat.

"How about a walk."

"Are you out of your tiny mind, it's pissing out there, and anyway I want to see how the dog makes out." You could count on one hand the number of times this man has walked without purpose in his life. We are not people who go for walks. But there he goes making a fuss, you know what they're like, and we hardly get any distance at all when he's stopped on the sidewalk trying to stare in through someone's drawn curtains. "Cut that out," I tell him. "Take a good look," he says, "You are looking at the heart of hearts of the free enterprise system." I pull at his sleeve and he comes along but slowly, turning his head back as if gawking is going to get us somewhere.

Next day I do a stir-fry, heavy on the sprouts, to keep him happy. I try to strike the right balance between cheap and good—something he will like to eat and something that isn't too expensive, since he pays for the groceries. And the heat, light, mortgage, etcetera. Not that he ever complains or anything, but I sure would like to make my contribution, fill up a cart and say, I'll get this. Or when the plumber came to fix the toilet where it was leaking around the base. The plumber said that the wax ring under the toilet had been squished. He said probably a very heavy man had sat on that toilet. I sucked in my gut a little nervously, but he said, "Wasn't you. Wasn't your husband. Don't you worry my lovey, I'll show you how I fix it, so you can do it next time." He was showing me how you undo the nuts at the base of the toilet and I was thinking, next time? I was thinking maybe some Very Heavy Man broke in during the night, used the bathroom, and then left. My husband had let the plumber in and then disappeared into his study, I could hear the computer clicking. He's a freelance investment consultant, I don't really understand it myself but he's got a fax in there, a couple of computers; he seems to do pretty well, every now and then he gets dressed up and goes to meet a client but it's mostly over the phone. So when the plumber told me it was done and he'd be on his way I sure would have liked to write him a cheque instead of calling up to my husband to come down. A couple of hours later I might say casually, Oh, the plumber, yeah, I took care of that.

At aerobics I notice Lisa has a snappy new pair of pants, white spandex with some impressive multicoloured foliage on them.

"Great pants, Lis, where'd you get those?"

"I went up to Marco and I told him straight out, If you don't do something nice and unexpected for me very soon, I'm leaving you. And he went out and bought me a pair of pants."

"Wow." What nerve. "Wow. Tell me again." So when I get home I march right up to my husband. "If you don't do something nice and unexpected for me soon, I might, well you never know, um, take off." And he says "Whereya going? Heheh." So I call Lisa.

"Did you look him right in the eye when you said it?" she asks.

"No."

"Well that's why." But she didn't mention anything about eyes up until that moment.

I'm snuggling deep down under the covers when my feet touch something hard and scrunchy.

"What's that?"

"Look and see." There's a package, heavy and all wrapped up in fancy paper and he says "That's enough talk of leaving," and it occurs to me that it doesn't look much like clothes but I say thank you anyway and give him a big smacker.

"Are you going to open it now? Or am I supposed to lie here all night?" So I rip off the paper and it's a book with a big leafy picture on the front that reminds me of Lisa's pants, and the words Grow Your Own In The Home For Fun And Profit. First thing I think is God he wants me to start trafficking, but then I look and there are sections on flowers and small vegetables and whatnot, with a whole chapter on watercress.

"Well. Well, thanks a lot, really, it's very nice."

"Anytime. Never hurts to learn a thing or two about watercress, keep you out of the bars maybe." He throws a warm arm across my stomach and pulls the blanket over his head.

Lisa is a good person to talk to. She knows what's what. Lisa will take account of your whole world and spread it out where you can see it. If you're not sure which way to go on something, she'll decide for you. It's true that a month later she might lay things out all different, but she's always convincing at the time. So I nab her in the locker room after class; she's sitting on the bench pulling up her jeans. I say, "Lisa, I've been thinking about what has value in a relationship. What a person contributes in a couple that is, say, not financial. How you quantify those things." Lisa doesn't look the least bit surprised by this; she stands and zips her jeans in a definitive kind of way.

"That's all bullshit," she says. "You don't add up value like that. There are no units of value. Have you guys talked about this? When was the last time you went out for dinner? You need to demand that he take you out for dinner. Now don't even think about somewhere cheap, I mean a fabulous dinner. Then you talk to him."

At supper—a supper I made, not a fabulous one: wimp, wimp—he's talking about keeping up your fibre. "Everyone knows that now," he says, "it's in the paper all the time, how raw vegetables are anti-carcinogenic. All these people who used to load up on the red meat are going home with zucchinis bursting gloriously out of their trunks, as it were." I remind him about when he was watching TV the night before and he scowls and says there's nothing wrong with a few chips and suchlike once you've got the fibre in.

"How you getting on with that book?" he wants to know.

"Book. Oh yes. Absolutely."

"It's the containers," he says, "that are the problem. But Liu says you can get a grant from that crowd up on the hill."

"Containers? Who?"

"Liu." He looks down when I stare at him. Innocent crunching. "I happened by." He raises pale blue eyes big and round like he never heard anything worse than gosh in his life.

"Let me remind you. We've been here six years."

"I got a little behind on my neighbourliness, my lawn mower chat." There is a look you can use to indicate that you know someone has never mowed a lawn. I give him that look, and then hum the theme music from Jeopardy: "The name of the people who live next door. What is..." He passes the salad bowl and says, "Roughage?"

Something is happening. A man in a suit is sitting at the head of our kitchen table. I was out in the shed, trying to make myself useful, when my husband called me in; he makes the introductions and asks me to sit down. He is dressed the way he does when he goes to see a client, which seems a little intimidating when you're covered in sawdust.

Mr. Liu is not a small man; he is sitting on the chair with the rungs that keep coming unglued, and this makes me nervous. "Tea first," announces Mr. Liu and my husband shoots out of his chair and plugs in the kettle, zips through the cupboards and locates the teapot, fusses with spoons and cups and taps his foot rapidly on the floor while the water boils. No one says anything. When my husband has served up tea all round and sat back down, Mr. Liu looks at both of us and speaks again.

"You have summoned me here today to address this problem," he says. I glare at my husband, who keeps his eyes fixed on Mr. Liu. I kick him under the table. He makes a noise but turns it into a cough. "Allow me to tell you an enigmatic Chinese story. This, I think, is what you are expecting. I was bathing my son one day. His usual towel was in the laundry, and in its place I had a blue and white striped towel. As he was preparing to exit the bath, he told me that he did not like cabinets. I found this surprising. Cabinets? I repeated. You do not like cabinets? Yes, my son told me, he did not like stripy cabinets... You see the meaning of this, I think. The pertinence to your own situation." He looks at my husband.

"Certainly," says my husband quickly. Mr. Liu turns to me.

"I'm not sure that I quite, uh, I don't really understand what's going on here."

"This is OK." He looks me right in the eye. "The main thing is that you have value as a person. Yes. This is most important." For some reason, what Mr. Liu has said makes me feel intensely relieved. The feeling is something like sexual arousal, that sense of warmth spreading outward, only it's not sexual but peaceful, and it comes from somewhere in my upper back, between my shoulder blades. And my husband over there, looking a bit teed off that his value has not been mentioned thus far. Mr. Liu turns to him. "As for you, remember that if the cabinet door is locked, you will not be able to open it."

"I thought it was supposed to be a towel," says my husband sourly.

"Now. I believe it is time for the gifts." Something rings; Mr. Liu takes a cell phone from the pocket inside his suit jacket and opens it. "Please excuse me a moment." He walks into the living room.

"How was I supposed to get him a present?" I hiss. "I've never seen this man before. Why didn't you tell me he was coming?"

"Do not be alarmed," says Mr. Liu, returning to the kitchen. He produces a large briefcase from beside his chair, sets it on the table, and pops it open. He withdraws two packages identically wrapped in shiny silver paper with purple ribbon. He hands one to my husband, who seems taken aback. "Please," he says. My husband opens it. The gift is a photograph in black and white of a golf course; it is possible to see in the distance something which could be a man cutting the grass. The course looks grey and mysterious, a place where things happen which have to do with matters far greater than clubs and little balls. My husband examines it carefully before nestling it back in the tissue paper. He grips Mr. Liu's hand and shakes it. Mr. Liu looks at me and I open my gift, which is a pair of denim overalls in my size from

Mark's Work Wearhouse. The fabric is thick and durable; there are several pockets. "Thank you," I say. "Thank you, Mr. Liu."

That more or less rounded off our encounter. Mr. Liu took another call on the cell and left quickly, saying he had an urgent appointment. They moved out of the neighbourhood not long after. When I saw the movers I went to my husband's study and knocked on the door. He pressed his thumb against his nose, spread his fingers apart and wiggled them at me. "Pay attention," I said. He stopped wiggling. I told him I wanted money enough to buy Mr. Liu an expensive housewarming present. He signed a cheque and gave it to me: "Go mad." I slipped the box into the back of the moving truck when no one was looking. There was no card, but a thank-you note appeared in our mailbox a few days later. We are still here.

Jim Maunder

Talking

*H*arry has just returned from walking Jeanie the few blocks to the Three Brothers Grocery and back home with fresh vegetables, Italian bread and pasta sauce. Vaughan Road, mostly populated by Italians and Caribbeans, slices through, at an odd angle, the neatly ordered upper-middle-class North York neighbourhoods above St. Clair Avenue near Bathurst Street. Jeanie never felt uncomfortable here before.

"Hey, Harry man, we having party. You come join us, and your lady."

The side yard is tumbling and spinning with children, their black faces and arms and knees strobing against their bright summer clothing. Their fathers and stepfathers, uncles and older male cousins all here to visit Uncle Thomas for the long weekend. Sitting and standing, drinking and laughing and arguing in the heat haze of Labour Day afternoon. The women are here too, inside preparing food. Harry can't quite pick out the spices but they sure smell good.

"Thanks, but I have to work, do some work in the..."

"Work another day, man! Come. My brother here from Montreal, my wife, children. Have a drink. We have plenty food."

"Maybe later, Thomas." Harry walks away. Walks to the brick shed out back and unlocks the door. This shed he shares with Thomas who lives alone in the basement apartment. The shed is included with the rent for the upstairs. It's the main reason Harry wanted this house. But Thomas was already renting downstairs and using the shed to store supplies for his kitchen and bathroom renovations business. Jeanie, and Pam who would be renting the other room, had scouted ahead, found the place while Harry was still home in Newfoundland finishing some work. Jeanie told him on the phone that Thomas was flirting with them. Thomas told Jeanie to tell her man to stay in New Finland, he'd look after her. She told Harry he seemed harmless enough. Kind of sweet really. He had been a perfect gentleman since Harry turned up. Seemed impressed that he was living with two women. Harry couldn't ask him to move out of the shed so they agreed to divide the space in half. Thomas would pay fifty dollars a month. He was never late.

Many warm evenings on the porch, Harry carving wood and Jeanie studying, Thomas would bring beer for them. Sit on the railing, telling them about his island off the coast of Madagascar. "It's beautiful there. Sun all the time. All the women beautiful. Yeah is true, all them. But no money. Here is money but so cold! In winter how you stand it?" Thomas always laughing. Offering a toast to everything. "You are true artist, Harry. Here's to your hands. Here's to your eyes. Here's to your vision. Jeanie is great student. Here's to your brain. Here's to your career." That's what Harry heard. Half of what Thomas said he couldn't understand at all. He'd try for a while and then just nod and smile.

Harry steps over the two-by-eights and moves back a sink, annoyed today at Thomas encroaching on his half. He turns on the oxygen and acetylene and fires up the torch. There's a half-life-sized drawing of a naked couple taped to the wall, the man lifting the woman to his waist, both gazing at their hands

Talking

entwined above their heads. A steel version of the drawing is emerging from the work bench as Harry heats and twists and welds in the dim light of one fluorescent tube and the open doorway.

Thomas walks in. Walks right up to Harry. "I invite you to have drink. Why you won't have drink with me and my family?"

Harry searches. Doesn't want to answer.

"Why you don't drink with me?"

"Okay." Harry sighs. "You remember at our party you said if I ever had a problem with you I should tell you?" Thomas at this party, drunk and loud. Standing at the toilet pissing with the door half open. A friend of Pam's, a big, beautiful black woman who makes hats, walks in. He says come in, come in, don't be shy, don't be shy, you like what you see? She gets upset. A cold ripple runs through the party and Thomas is feeling bad.

"Yeah I remember, sure."

"It's not you. But your cousin Michael..."

"What he do?"

"He's been making comments to Jeanie and Pam."

"What he saying?"

"Well for one thing, yesterday he walked right into the house, into the bedroom when Jeanie was alone. Said he wanted to use the phone, said she was beautiful and he'd love to sleep with her."

"You say these things. I don't understand you say. I get my brother. He know better English." Thomas rushes away. Harry stands staring at the sculpture, feeling his stomach falling, falling.

Christian comes in to hear Harry out. Harry says, "Thomas is really upset. I don't want to make a big deal about it, but Jeanie is nervous when Michael is around. I just want it to stop. That's all."

Christian says, "It's always best to clear the air. Thomas is drunk and when he is drunk he gets very emotional. Don't worry about it. I'll talk to Michael. I think you should come out and join us."

"In a little while. Thank you." They shake hands.

Harry relights his torch and is contemplating the curve of a thigh when the light from the door disappears. He turns to see Michael's huge form rimmed by sunlight. Michael steps in and closes the door. Harry keeps the torch lit. "Why you saying these things to Thomas? Shame me in front of my cousin? My wife? My children? What I do? You tell me what I do!" Michael moves towards Harry. Harry tightens his grip on the torch until Michael comes into the light. Until he sees his face, close to tears. "You tell me."

"The women are upset by your comments..."

"I only say they're beautiful. What is wrong? Women like that."

"You said more than that..."

"No. No."

"You told Jeanie you wanted to sleep with her."

"Come on. You're a man. You see a beautiful woman. You say you like to sleep with her."

"No. I don't."

"What kind of man are you? Where I'm from women like that. Expect that. Is just talking, man."

"Yeah? Well, okay, I can appreciate that. We have different cultures. But the women where I'm from..."

"What you going to do? Call police?" Michael is more agitated now. Harry grips the torch a little tighter again.

"No. No, listen. Like I said, I can appreciate it if that's what you are used to, I just want you to know that Jeanie and Pam don't like it and I just want you to not do that any more. I'm sorry about Thomas. I thought he would just talk to you."

"He drunk. He shoot off his mouth to everyone. Very bad for me. My wife not speaking to me."

"I'm sorry about how this came out...but Thomas kept asking why I wouldn't join you. It needed to be cleared up. I'll try to smooth it over with Thomas, but I've said I appreciate your position and if you can appreciate mine then let's shake hands and move on, can we?" Harry extinguishes the torch.

Michael, somewhat resigned, extends his hand and holds on to Harry's grip. "You say we're okay, then you come out and have a drink with us. Show them we're okay."

"All right I will. I just have to shut this stuff down." Michael leaves. Harry punches himself in the forehead; thinks, good timing, asshole. Ruin the whole weekend for Thomas and his entire family, why don't you? Shit! Why can't I keep my mouth shut?

Harry comes out into the yard, now full of women and children and food. Chicken, potatoes, salad, bread. Christian is there but Thomas and Michael can be heard in the basement arguing in an African-French patois. Christian sits Harry down in a lawn chair. "Stay here. I'll get you a drink." He returns with a beer glass full of clear liquid. Harry takes a sip. Bacardi? Soda, maybe, but not much. A woman brings him a huge plate of food.

"Oh. Thanks, but that's too much. I'll be having supper soon."

"Eat. Eat!"

Christian sits with him. Tells him about his club in Montreal. "I'm the owner and the DJ. We have social nights for Africans, but for everyone. Lots of music and food and dancing. Very good vibes. You should come by if you are in Montreal. Here's my card." African Vibes Social Club.

Harry is eating. Getting drunk too fast. Trying to figure how to waste some of the drink on the grass without being noticed. Thomas comes out. Comes over to Harry. "So you join us. That's good. That's good. You have enough food? How's your drink?"

Jeanie comes around the corner. The sun is low and backlights her hair with a copper glow and silhouettes her long legs through her thin cotton dress. She is the only person in the yard unaware of this. She is also the only one, except perhaps for some of the children, unaware of the messy scene that's been unfolding. The women stare through her clothes, dissecting her tempting white flesh with their dark eyes. The men's eyes treat it with a kinder passion. Jeanie says, "Hi Harry, I came to tell you supper was ready but I see you're already taken care of." Thomas tells her to have some food and she says, "Oh. Okay. It looks great." She digs in, laughs. "So are these all your kids, Thomas?"

He laughs too. "No, no. Not all these."

"How many do you have?"

"Ah, ten. But just these two, here. With this woman. Some more in Montreal. Some more in Africa."

"And you're how old?"

"Thirty-two."

"You've been busy." They laugh again.

Harry holds his face in his hands, tries to keep his head from spinning. He thinks, she has no idea. My great chivalry. Huh. Patronizing, that's how she'll see it. Like there's a difference. He shivers. Realizes the evening has clouded in. A few pecks of rain. The garden has been gradually emptying, the food cleared, the chairs folded. He makes his way to Jeanie and Thomas who are still chatting easily. "I guess we better get in, eh? I think it's going to rain. Thanks for the food. It was great. And the big drink." He smiles, raises his glass to Thomas, and swallows down the last of it.

. . .

Harry sits in the kitchen and tells Jeanie about the confrontation.

"Thanks," she says, "I guess."

Harry shakes his head and stares at the floor. "My god. What did I do?"

"Hey." Jeanie lifts her dress and straddles his lap, kisses his lips and laughs. "My hero."

Michael Winter

Archibald the Arctic

*E*arly on New Year's Day my mother woke me to say, calmly, that two police officers were at the door. She said this in the same way she'd say there's a fried egg sandwich in the oven. I was seventeen, home for Christmas, staying in Junior's room, in his bed in fact. I had been out with Geoff Doyle and Skizicks the night before, we ended up on Crow Hill throwing our empties down on the tracks, enjoying the wet distant crumple they made, waiting for the fireworks to sputter into the cold dark air. I remember Skizicks, who is a year older and knew we were virgins, saying he'd screwed Heidi Miller against the wall in behind Tim Horton's. Over the course of two long minutes we counted the reports of eleven shotguns, sounding small, disorganized and lonely.

I walked to the porch in my cold jeans, barefoot. I was hungry and my head hurt. I worked my mouth. The police officers were still outside. I opened the screen door. The white metal handle was frosty. Snow was drifting lightly onto their new fur hats, their epaulets, sliding off the waxed cruiser which hummed quietly in behind my father's car. There were no lights flashing. The driveway needed to be shovelled. Doyle would be up in his window, if he was up. The officers were facing each other, conversing. Their footprints were the first to our door in the new year. They looked fit and very awake.

Are you Gabriel English?

Yes.

We have a warrant for your arrest, son.

I knew there was something you could say here. I searched for the proper wording.

Can I ask what the charge is?

We'll discuss that at the station.

Am I under arrest?

This is what my father had taught us. When the law wants you, ask if you're under arrest. I was glad I could remember it.

We'd prefer to formally charge you down at the station, son, after we've cleared a few things up.

My father, who had been in the bathroom shaving, came to the door. He was still in his undervest, mopping his neck and chin with a white towel. He wasn't wearing his glasses, which gave him a relaxed look. He said, Would it be all right, fellas, if the boy had some breakfast? I'll bring him down right after.

The way he dried himself with the towel showed off his massive, pale biceps, his thick wrists. The thickness was well-earned. There was a beat and then the older officer said that would be fine. He decided to look at my father for a moment and then they turned and made new footprints back to the cruiser.

My father turned to me and said, Well what a way to start the new year. He said this in a way that reassured me. He knew already that I hadn't done anything, that I wasn't capable of doing a bad thing. He was confident about this, all he knew about me was good things. I was the good son. His impression reinforced a faith in my own innocence. It made me realize what must have happened and suddenly I got upset.

It's Junior, isn't it, he said.

I suspect it's Junior, Dad.

And why do you suspect him.

He knew that I must be in league with Junior, had information that we'd kept from him. Over breakfast I told him what I knew. He listened as if, while the particulars of the event were new to him, they fit into the larger maze which was the interlaced lives of his sons. He said, They're going to begin with a presumption. That you've been driving. And you haven't. Be flat out with that and the rest hold to your chin. He said, People in charge like to figure things out. They don't appreciate confessions.

We drove to the police station, which was a bunker below the Sir Richard Squires building. The building housed the first elevator in Newfoundland.

I liked the Up and Down arrows by the elevator buttons. That was my earliest appreciation of technology's ability to appear prescient. I thought it was a considerate touch by the makers. The elevator was the avenue to Corner Brook's public library, which my father had introduced to me before I could read. I would pick up books Junior had chosen, like *Archibald the Arctic* and stare at the riddle of print. Junior loved the northern explorers — of men eating their dogs, and then each other.

The lobby was glass on three sides, with nine storeys of brick pressing down on it. My father took me to the sixth floor once, to a government office where he had some tax business. I could see the Bowater mill, the neck of the bay twisting around the town of Curling, the swans (the whitest things in town) drifting below in the reservoir which cooled the mill's furnaces, the secondary schools on the landscaped hill to the east. I was uneasy in the building. I was convinced the glass footing would topple. I worried for the commissionaire stationed at his desk by the fountain.

The fountain stood in the centre of the lobby behind an iron railing. It drizzled water over its scalloped and flared glass edges.

A boy was carefully tossing a penny in. The fountain was a silent, enormous presence, a wordless example of grander things one could value and live for. I loved the fountain even when no one and nothing told me it was worthy of love.

My father leaned against the rail. He said if he had guts, he'd sell everything and help the poor in Calcutta. That was his base belief about what was right. His weakness drove him to self-interest, to preserving family and constantly bettering our material position. He could appreciate decorative flourishes, but never allowed himself to get carried away.

My mother would say I have these thoughts because we emigrated from England. My mother has given a lot of time to such considerations. She cultivates hindsight, and researches the repercussions of certain acts. Perhaps if I had grown up where I was born, had not felt strange in my own skin, I wouldn't be so sensitive in the world. In the house I spoke with an English accent, outside I pronounced words the way Doyle and Skizicks said them. I said brakfest, chimley, sove you a seat. I was aware of the boundary between blood bond and friends, between house and world. Junior was different. He managed to be pure Newfoundlander.

My father and I walked down to the police station and I began my brief story of never having driven a Japanese car in Alberta and the officer nodded as if he knew the truth of the matter only too well, that my arrest was a technicality, that a million brothers a month pretend to be younger brothers and he was going to add this latest infraction to the pile. I was free to go.

The station, below the library, was a place I had been to only once before, when Doyle and Skizicks and I were accused of breaking a window. We were kicking stones down Valley Road and a neighbour's window crashed in. We ran. We ran home. Junior said, When you're in trouble, where do you run?

Home.

No Gabe, always run away from home.

I found the station small and casual. It didn't look hard to break out of. There were three cells in the back that I could only hear.

I never spoke to Junior about this arrest. He had left to go back to Alberta on Boxing Day. He was plugging dynamite holes in Fort MacMurray.

My father has cried twice — once when a German shepherd we had ran from his knee and was crushed by a snow plough, the other when Junior left to work in the tar sands. It doesn't hurt me to think of him crying for Junior and not for my departure, or even crying for a dog we rescued from the pound, a thin, shivering creature who knew who to thank for fattening him up. He became too fierce in protecting us. Crying is an irrational act and should never be resented. I know Junior's life is a riskier thing. I know that my parents trust my good senses (I am named executor of their wills). There will be greater love attached to wilder men.

Before Christmas I went out with Junior to a cabin belonging to one of the Brads. Junior knew three men named Brad, and my mother had begun to disbelieve him. That the Brads had other names. She would answer the phone and say, No, he's off somewhere with one of the Brads. As if that was a joke and she wasn't to be fooled. But I believe they were all called Brad. I think perhaps naming someone Brad is not a good idea.

Brad picked us up in his black and gold Trans Am and tried his best to charm our mother who appreciated the gesture but still kept her opinion. I sat in the back and we detoured down

Mountbatten Road. We stopped at a house with blue aluminum siding. Brad honked his horn and a screen door opened with two women waving and smiling and pointing a finger to indicate one moment. Brad popped the trunk from inside and waited.

Me: Who are they.

Junior: Our wool blankets.

The girls climbed in the back and I remembered Linda from a party Junior had at the house. She had come into my bedroom, sat on the floor with a beer, and told me how she loved Junior to bits.

They nudged me with their hips to get their seat belts on. I was in the middle. Then Linda smiled: You're gonna be our chaperon, Gabe. Danielle leaned forward and pulled on Brad's hair and kissed him on the ear and I could see the perfect contour of her breast.

Brad Pynn had a cabin up in Pynn's Brook. Junior liked to go snowmobiling and drinking up there over the holidays. He'd flown into town, gotten his presents giftwrapped by Linda at the hardware store he used to work at, and invited her to Brad's.

Brad and Junior had an old plan to rob the small bank above Co-op grocery on Main Street. I don't mind revealing this because, to my knowledge, they never pulled the heist and now, I believe, the bank is closed. It was a small bank, used by members of the Co-op. It was less formal than other banks. There were just desks, rather than counters with glass. You could walk right into the safe if you were quick. Junior was convinced you could pull off that job. The only problem was, everyone knew him. And if you did it with someone like a Brad Pynn, you could never be sure if he'd blow too much money one night, or brag, or betray you.

This bank scheme was something that always came up after a few beers, or during a vial of oil and a sewing needle, which Junior had out in the front seat, spreading the green oil over a cigarette paper on his knee. The joint was passed and I had to take it from Danielle, smoke, and hand it to Linda. Danielle kept pressing my knee saying Look at that, if she saw a cute house, or a crow on the melted road that refused to lift. She'd press my knee then slide her hand a little up my thigh, as though she'd forgotten it was my thigh. Linda put her arm along the back window to make more shoulder room. They were quite relaxed.

Junior had a sawed-off shotgun between his legs which I watched him load with a red number four shell. He asked Brad to roll down his window. Cold air pummelled into the car. Junior clicked the chamber closed. He lifted the barrel up to Brad's windowsill, pushed off the safety, stared back at us and said, Watch this.

He saw Danielle's hand on my thigh and Linda's arm around my neck and paused.

There were three black objects ahead standing in the snow on Brad's side of the highway. Brad kept the speedometer at the limit. Junior didn't aim, just pointed at the grade and estimated the distance. He fired and the crows flew up alertly. Brad swerved.

Jesus, June.

He slipped off the road, hit bare ice, fishtailed, adjusted for the swing, pumped the brakes a little, and straightened up. The blast echoed inside the car. Junior was laughing until he saw that Linda and Danielle were horrified. We all saw, through a thin veil of trees, a line of cabins.

Oh, honey. Sorry about that.

Linda clenched her jaw and stared out her window. Her arms crossed and flexed.

Brad owned a Gold Wing which he parked and chained into the cabin over winter, and this bike he straddled and drank beer from and turned on the stereo embedded in the ruby fibreglass windjammer and would have started it up if Junior hadn't, at Brad's request, drained the cylinders and cleaned his valves and left the engine to hibernate in drenched oil.

Brad and June took the purple Arctic Cat for a bomb down the lake to ice fish and to hunt with the sawed-off. They carried a small auger and they had slugs in case of a moose. The girls and I played Scrabble and drank rum mixed with Tang crystals. I missed touching their arms and hips. They were about twenty, both attending the Career Academy and slowly becoming disappointed. But that winter they were still bright, talkative Newfoundland women who wore friendship rings and small twinkling earrings and could imagine ways to have fun and succeed. They'd spent summers working in the fish plant in Curling and winters wearing white skates on ponds like Little Rapids. I could tell they enjoyed me and while each on her own might have been bored with my company, together they shared a glee in flirting, in egging me on. In their eyes I was a man in the making, and I accepted this. Women like a confidence no matter what the confidence is.

Linda said, You're going to be something, aren't you. You're like your brother, but you're smarter and gentle.

Ah Linda he's shy, boy.

And Danielle put her arm around my neck and felt my ear. Her collarbone lifted a white bra strap. Shy? Why you got nothing to be shy about.

She slipped her hand down to my waist.

Have you ever done the dirty? she said.

I didn't have to answer and they laughed and loved the fact that now they were getting into this.

You know something me and Linda have wanted to do? Linda felt my crotch. She put a hand in my jeans pocket.

Wow. Danielle. Guess what he's not wearing.

Go way.

Danielle slipped her hand in my other pocket. This pocket had the lining torn and her warm, probing hand clasped directly and gently.

Oh Linda we've got a fine young man on our hands.

A growing boy.

Linda unbuttoned my jeans. I shifted in my chair and prayed that the skidoo would be loud. I tried to recall the sound it made as it buzzed up the lake. But as it was, even if Brad and Junior came in the door, nothing could be seen above the table. Nothing except an astonished boy and two eager, laughing women leaning in to him.

Last fall Junior hit a moose. This was six days after the mandatory seat belt law had been established, and it was this law which had saved his life. Dad and I found him unconscious, pinned behind the wheel of his orange-and-chrome VW Bug. Eight hundred pounds of moose had rolled over the bonnet, crumpled the windshield, bent the doorframes and lay bleeding in his lap. The ambulance service had to wait for the jaws of life to free him. He'd loved the Bug, it had lived its previous life in salt-free Florida. Investigators measured skid marks, the animal was towed off with two canvas cables, its injuries charted, witnesses signed statements and it was declared that Junior had been driving with abandon under severe winter conditions.

He bought a Rabbit then, and two weeks later he rammed into the back of an eighteen-wheeler; the Rabbit was dragged four hundred metres before the semi braked. The trucker was furious, he hadn't even seen Junior he was that far up his ass. Up your wind tunnel, Junior said, looking for an opportunity to pass. The trucker wanted to smack him. He would have if my father hadn't stretched his big hands in an obvious way.

Junior began giving up on a Datsun, an old, whipped car. He was motoring around town, scouting for other drivers' infractions. Someone running a red light. If he saw anything, he drove into it. He was making money, he said, from other people's insurance.

When the Datsun had built up a nest egg he asked if I wanted to go for a ride. This was after supper, in early December. He'd decided, he said, to retire the vehicle. The insurance company had declared it a liability and he had to write it off before the calendar year.

We drove to the empty, carefully ploughed parking lot behind the school my father taught at. The street lamps were just flickering on. It was terminally ill, Junior said, and we had to put it out of its misery.

He revved up the motor, spun on the slightly icy pavement, and swaggered the car towards a ploughed mound of snow at the edge of the lot.

Hold on, Gabe.

The headlights lurched, grew in concentration against the bank as we accelerated and approached. The car exploded into compact snow, driving in a few feet, snow smacking against the windshield, the hill absorbed our blow. The motor muffled, hummed, still ran happily. If it had a tail it would be wagging.

Junior shifted into reverse, hit the wipers, spun wide, and galloped for the opposite end of the lot, dipsy doodling around a street-light pole on the way, swinging on the ice and slamming sideways into the far bank of snow.

I had to get out and push this time. The exhaust was clogged with snow. I watched as Junior aimed for a sturdier bank pressed against the school. The car whined horribly. There was no give in the snow. The seat belt cut against his chest as he came up hard on a hidden concrete post. A crease formed in the hood of the car, the grill burst open and jets of water spouted up, dousing the windshield and melting then freezing the snow on the hood.

The motor kept running as if nothing had happened. I ran to him.

Can't kill a fucking Datsun, man.

Junior got out to reconsider his approach. I reminded him that if he went through with this demolition we'd have to walk home. He popped the hood (it opened at the windshield) and cranked up the heat to transfer valuable degrees over from the engine. Then he said, Come look at this.

We stood on the front bumper and stared into the dark classroom. On the board were the yellow chalk drawings our father made of various projects: tables, lamps, chairs. There were angles and choice of wood screw and the correct use of a plane and a clamp. The work tables were cleared, the tools all hanging in their racks, the cement floor swept with sawdust and water. Everything in order.

We drove home with the broken radiator, my eyes fixed to the temperature gauge, which hovered past the orange bar.

It was then Junior asked me for a favour. We were parked, the lights shut off, the engine ticking to the cold. He said his insurance was sky-high. What we'd do, he said, is insure his next car in my name and he'd be a second driver. It would save him a hell of a lot of cash.

At the time I wasn't driving anything and when you're not using something, it's hard to feel the importance of giving it away. There was a mature air about Junior needing my help in the adult world. But a warning hunch spread through my body. I knew there would be repercussions, though I could not articulate them. It all seemed reasonable, he just needed to borrow my driver's license for an hour.

It wasn't just the insurance, the police told me. The car was registered in my name too. I had an overdrawn bank account. There was a bad prairie loan. A lien on a leased Ford pickup. In Alberta, his entire life had become my life. He was living under the name Gabriel English. It was as if he never expected me to live a life, so he'd better do it for me.

Jim Maunder

Rust

*T*revor guns the big engine and his red '76 Camaro skitters up the steep gravel driveway. He veers to the left and parks on the grassy clearing by his sister's log house. As he's unloading his weekend bag and groceries, Katie comes skipping from the house. Trevor scoops her up in his free arm and kisses her nose and she giggles. Anne follows Katie. Group hug. Katie runs off to join another small girl playing with a woman on a blanket at the far side of the clearing. Trevor stares, "Who's that?"

"That's Rose. And her little girl, Melody. They came out for the weekend too. I told her about you. She's looking forward to meeting you."

"I've seen her before."

"Careful little brother. She's special."

"You know I'm harmless."

"I know. What happened after with Susan?"

"That didn't go anywhere. I think she went out with me to be polite. Not to offend a young brother-in-the-cause. Anyway, where did you find them?"

"The girls started playing together in the park. We've been getting together whenever Katie and I are in town. She needed to get away from her family for a while. Come over and meet them."

"Is there a Melody's father or..."

"Nope."

When they reach the blanket, Rose is on her back, the two three-year-olds on top of her, laughing and tickling. She roars and tickles them back, her bare feet stirring the air. Trevor steals a glance as her long Indian cotton skirt slips down, in slow motion, the hem lightly tracing the smooth, tanned contours of her thighs. She brushes her hair from her face and looks up with big moist eyes, like a whitecoat on a poster, Trevor thinks, but smiling, smiling eyes yet he can easily imagine them sorrowful, like a whipped puppy.

"Hello. I guess you're Trevor," then she laughs a muffled laugh as Katie plops down on her face. "Aarrgh! Hey Trevor could you help me here?"

Trevor lifts Katie off, careful not to brush against Rose's breasts as he does, thinking how soft and welcoming they look under her thin cotton shirt. He holds his niece stiffly, not knowing what to do next. But Katie and Melody conspire with a glance and tackle him, knocking him off balance. He lands in Rose's lap. The two little girls tickle him and squeal. Rose composes herself and calms them. Anne asks for help with supper and the girls run along to the house with her.

Trevor picks a tall piece of timothy grass and twirls it between his fingers. He is unable to think of anything to say. Even the part of his brain that can always be counted upon to find some witticism, some pun or obscure connection to distract and steady him in times of stress, is struck dumb in the presence of this woman.

Finally, Rose says, "Hey Trevor, Anne has been telling me about the Fairy Trail. Can you show me?" They walk through the woods on an old moose path, the late afternoon sunlight trickling through the dense overhang, casting its aura around pale green old man's beard and huge speckled mushrooms growing from ancient tree stumps. "Do you think Melody is a silly name?"

"No. It's beautiful, like her. It suits her." Then, "She sure does look like you."

Trevor turns a little red and Rose laughs, "Thanks." Further on, Rose asks, "Do you hear waterfalls?"

"Yeah, see down there?" He points down a steep embankment, through a thick stand of birch trees, "That's Anne's skinny-dipping pool. See the falls? Sometimes there's trout that bump against your legs."

"God, it's so pretty!"

Trevor, feeling braver, "She has a sign down there—No swimsuits allowed."

"Oh yeah? We'll have to come back here when it's warmer."

Trevor's heart pounds like it hasn't since he was hit by a car when he was seven. His eardrums are timpani.

Saturday dawns cold and foggy and the day is spent playing games with the kids, all hands preparing a vegetarian feast of dolmades, spanokapita and Greek salad, and Rose curled up in a chair reading Anne's notebook full of poetry. Sunday, with Trevor's hopes of slipping off to the waterfalls with Rose fading, he gives her a conspiratorial smile, "I wish it would warm up out there."

"I don't. I'm just enjoying being in a house that's peaceful for a change. And it's giving me a chance to get to know Anne better." She goes back to her reading.

It's decided that Trevor will drive Rose and Melody back to town. As they're loading up, Melody inspects the Camaro. "Your car got spots."

Rose laughs, "Yeah. It looks like when you had chicken pox, Sweety."

"I've been working on it most weekends all summer," says Trevor, a bit defensive. "when I get the time. I hope to get it painted soon."

"That'd be good. It's cute this way, though."

They sing most of the way out the Salmonier Line to the highway. There Was an Old Woman Who Swallowed a Fly, Mares Eat Oats and Does Eat Oats, Bobby Magee, until Melody falls asleep.

"So what do you do when you're not painting spots on your car?"

"Well, a lot. I work at Sears doing display. It's like window dressing but there's no windows."

"That's kinda neat."

"Mmm. It's sort of artistic but it's not what I want to do for long. I'm taking art classes at the University Extension. And a writing class, poetry."

"Do classes cost a lot?"

"Yeah, they do a bit. What about you? What do you do when you're not taking care of spots on Melody?"

"I hang out with her. That's full-time. I like it, she's a cool kid. But I draw and write poetry too. I've got books full of it. It's not as good as Anne's but..."

"I'd love to see them sometime."

"Maybe someday. I never show them to anybody."

"What are you doing next weekend?"

"Me and Melody are going on the No Nukes march."

"Yeah? I helped organize that, with Ploughshares Youth. Actually I remember seeing you there last year."

"There was a lot of people there. You remember me?"

"I do. I couldn't believe it when I saw you at Anne's."

"I don't remember you..."

There's a silence. Trevor turns on the radio. Top ten. The Police are number one. He sings along, "Every step you take, every move you make, I'll be watching you."

This had become their song although, of course, she didn't know it. With all the song's attendant guilt, frustration and longing, since seeing her at last year's No Nukes and more intensely since the stirring of spring, he had searched for her. He had been with other women but he was thinking of her and so had lost interest in them. It wasn't just physical, he told himself. It was the softness in her manner, her flowing hippie clothing, her gentle way with her daughter. On some level he was aware that she was the embodiment of all his fantasies, and as such, could not be real. But he was consumed with the ideal of her. So much so that when they did happen to be in the same coffee shop, the same bookstore, he had frozen, unable even to make eye contact.

Trevor turns down the radio. "It's amazing how much we have in common."

"I guess. In some ways."

"What do you mean? Everything we've talked about, and I mean you're a friend of Anne's so...she thinks you're really special, you know."

Rose studies his face. "There's something I don't get. You're this nice, gentle, long-haired, left-wing hippie dude, right? So what's with the muscle car?"

"Oh, yeah, that. My last car fell apart. My friend Brian from work was helping me pick out another one 'cause I don't know much about cars. This one was the daily special. Brian wanted to drive it. Got it up to a hundred and sixty on the arterial. I thought the salesman would freak but he was pretty cool. Anyway, Brian somehow talked me into buying it. It's been a good car except for the rust. But I keep thinking I should get rid of it. Trade it in on a Volvo or something."

"I don't know. It's kinda sexy."

"Oh. Anyway what do you mean we only have stuff in common in some ways?"

"You have money."

"Money's not important."

"It's important when you got none."

"Anyway, I don't have much money. I have an old car and I still have to live at home with my parents."

"Yeah but Anne showed me your parent's home. It's huge."

"I guess, but we were always the poor ones in our neighbourhood."

"Us too, but you should see my neighbourhood."

Trevor drops them off at the end of a densely populated row of low-income housing, throbbing with kids and bikes and dogs and revving vehicles in varying states of repair and disrepair. Graffiti on the fences and on the walls, and not a tree to be seen. Trevor's anti-poverty advocacy calling trumpets loudly and he feels vital. "Can I call you?"

"No, you can't."

"...Oh."

"Oh, no, sorry. It's just, we don't have a phone. But you're welcome to drop by anytime. We like you." Melody gives him a big grin.

After three days, too distracted to work, Trevor gathers the courage to drop by. The house is full. Rose introduces him to her brothers. Don comes in from outside. He's the oldest at twenty-four, then there's her, then Rick and Jeff and Mary who's thirteen. Their mother is out and Melody is in bed. There are a few friends and girlfriends there. The Price is Right is on loud, and the air is thick with tobacco and hash smoke, hops and sweat socks.

"What do you do, Don?"

"Nudding. You?"

"I work at Sears."

"Oh! A working man?" Don as Elvis, "Well thank you. Thank you very much"

"For what?"

"Taxes."

"What do you mean?"

"Well, see my grandfather fought in the war so that people like you would have the freedom to pay taxes and people like me would have the freedom to do nudding. It's my patriotic duty not to let him down, see?"

"I see."

"Hey don't get your face all wrinkly there, buddy, I work when I can, cut wood and shit like that, can't get a real job. Quit school to help support the family when Dad fucked off, good old Newfoundland story, right? The rest of us, well except for Gary, he's between me and Rose, he's in jail, but he was never quite all there anyway, not his fault, but the rest of us are all here. Gotta stick together. We're family, right? "

"I can respect that."

"Oh good. That makes me feel much better knowing a fine fella like you respects me. I feel much better now." He claps Trevor's shoulder, "Hey I'm just yankin' your chain. Just fuckin' with ya, right? You're probably one of the good ones. Anyways, Rose seems to like ya so you can't be all bad. You gotta watch her though, she's a bit of a slut." Rose slaps his arm and he laughs, wraps his arm tight around her neck. "Nice car you got there. '76, 350, four barrel, right?"

"Yeah."

"I was noticing your bodywork. You could use a few more passes with finer grit. A hundred, then one-twenty at least. I can give you a hand if you want."

"Thanks, but I'm nearly done."

"Not really. Anyway, have a beer, b'y. And there's a draw around here somewhere. Hey, asshole, pass that over here will ya? We got company." He smacks his little brother on the head and hands Trevor the joint. Trevor fills his lungs.

At the end of the evening, Rose hugs Trevor at the door, "Do you want some company at the march?"

Rose and Melody are waiting on the step when Trevor comes by to drive them downtown. They join the crowd of about two hundred at City Hall. Teenagers in tie-dye, mothers, fathers, children in hand and in backpacks, university professors, grandparents. Speakers from groups such as Physicians for Nuclear Disarmament and Oxfam preach to the converted but the sun is shining and everyone is in a good mood. The march to the park is boisterous. Songs and chants and banners waving. Trevor and Rose laugh at the curious and the dirty looks they catch from passersby.

Trevor can hardly believe his luck. This gorgeous woman walking by his side, apparently enjoying his company. The world doesn't sort itself out this way. Women like that don't go for an ordinary guy like him. Not unless there's something wrong with them. Their self-esteem or their eyesight. Another day he would have settled for that conclusion. But today was so right, the sun and the singing, he was willing to concede that maybe there was something right with him.

Seven women sing The Times They Are a Changin' from the stage. Trevor hoists Melody to his shoulders, sways her to the music and tips his head back to sing to her. She drums on his forehead and giggles. Rose says, "You'd make a great father."

Trevor searches her face for deeper meaning but she takes his hand and pulls them toward the tent stalls. "Let's get cotton candy!"

Trevor treats. They sit under a tree, their lips blue and sticky. Rose says, "I don't even like the taste that much. But I can't go to a fair without getting some."

"I like it."

"I know you do, Sweety!"

"Do you? Like it, Twevah?"

"Yeah. It's not bad. I never had it before."

"Are you serious, Trevor? Huh! I think it's the smell. For me. You know? Whenever I smell it I get this flashback of one time my father took us all to the fair in Corner Brook when we were still living in Buchans. I was about Melody's size I guess and I'd never seen anything like it before. There was clowns and rides and cotton candy and that day I can remember thinking the world could be perfect. It's the smell of it brings that back."

Beer and dope and T.V. become the routine for Trevor at Rose's every few nights. The same crowd is there again tonight. Melody is in bed and her grandmother is out as usual. Rose won't leave her with anyone else—"Bunch of drunks and dopeheads." So they stay in and join the party, partaking as much as the rest of them.

Don screeches to a stop outside and comes in with more beer. "Where's the Camaro, man? You wreck her or what?"

"No, I left it home so I wouldn't. Walked up."

Don is drunk. He grabs Rose hard around the shoulders. "What's the matter, Rosie? Your boyfriend can't hold his beer?"

"Shag off, asshole! If you had half the sense he has...oh forget it. You wouldn't understand."

"No. No. I respect that! I respect that!"

"Don, you fuckin' jerk."

"Okay. You're right, Rosie. When you're right, you're right. Trevor, please accept this beer as a token of my apologies. Shall we carry on as if we were normal?"

Trevor accepts.

Rose sees him to the door around one-thirty. She hugs him long and tight. Trevor, not wanting to be the first to let go, "I'd love to stay longer but I do have to work tomorrow."

"You go on. You're the first person I've known with the sense to keep a job." She pecks him on the lips and releases her grip. Trevor wants more but he's far too unsure of himself and afraid of speeding a rejection to push the issue. He pecks her back and leaves.

Trevor calls Anne to talk about it. She says Rose considers him a dear friend. He hates the way that sounds.

Saturdays and Sundays Trevor spends in coveralls, goggles and dust mask, chasing the shade in a circle around his mother's front yard maple tree, moving the car along a few feet each hour. Occasionally with Don's help, or with Rose lounging and Melody running wild in the tall grass. The Monroes are the tolerated oddballs of Darby Place, artists, with a deliberately unmanicured garden, unrestrained dandelion seeds annually violating all the surrounding upper-middle-class lawns. Trevor revels in the scruffy shade-tree mechanic image, waving at the stuffiest of CEO neighbours every chance he gets.

An afternoon in August, Trevor rings Rose's doorbell five or six times with no response. As he's heading back home through the path beside her backyard, he hears music and hoists himself up to look in. Rose is lying face down on a towel. Trevor's panoramic view of the sun's light reflecting off the length of her slender brown back and legs is punctuated only by one small bright blue triangle. He says hello and she sits up, her breasts heavy and glistening with sweat. An image of water balloons darts ridiculously through his mind as she lazily scoops herself up into her blue bikini top. "Oh, hi," she says, sleepily, "What time is it?" His pulse beats so loud in his ears he barely hears her say she has to go, a friend is taking her to look at an apartment.

Trevor doesn't see Rose for over three weeks. Whenever he goes by her mother's place, if there's anyone there at all, they don't know or don't much seem to care where she is. He finishes the bodywork, leaving two concentric circles worn in the grass around the maple. He has the car painted silver, against Brian's advice, and the metallic surface emphasizes every imperfection in his sanding. As much as this frustrates him, he doesn't do any more repairs. His every free moment is spent driving around Bannerman Park and other places she might be.

The Police are still number one on the car radio. He starts to worry that he's become obsessed. He feels isolated and uneasy. But then, it's just that she doesn't have a phone, isn't used to them. Or she would have called by now. There's no question that she likes him. Women always *like* him, he's fucking sick of it. If he could only get his nerve up to make a move, maybe that's all she's waiting for. A little backbone.

He does catch a glimpse of her once, walking in the other direction by Scamper's Take Out, walking with some guy so he doesn't stop and turn the car around. He's not even sure it's her but he feels sick in his stomach. He'd always calculated how much in love he was by how sick he felt.

Eventually, Trevor sees Rose pushing Melody on a park swing and pulls the Camaro into the parking lot. He strolls over as if he's found them by accident. They both seem glad to see him. "Hi Trevor. We haven't seen you in a while." Rose hugs him and he holds on.

"I didn't know where you were," his voice quaking, "I missed you."

"You got it painted finally, hey? Not bad. We were just going home but it's a long walk. You wanna give us a ride in your shiny new chick-mobile?"

The second floor of a semidetached in a rundown section of Hamilton Avenue. Daylight barely finds its way through the few small windows. Weary institutional yellow walls and a vague musty smell throughout. "God I love it here." She puts one hand on his arm, the other she holds up to stop the world, "Just listen to that quiet." After a moment of silence, "I'd ask you to stay for supper but there's hardly any food." Trevor orders pizza. While they're waiting Rose tells him she's started upgrading at the trades college to get her high school diploma. Now that she's got somewhere peaceful to study. Would he help her with her math homework?

They finish the pizza and put Melody to bed. The geometry is a struggle. Trevor was good at it in high school but it's been a few years. Rose gets most of it, then says, "Fuck it. That's enough for tonight. You want some tea?"

"Did you want me to get some beer?"

"No. I'm off it."

"Sure, I'd love to have some tea with you. How are you liking school, anyway, besides the geometry?"

While they drink their tea, Rose tells Trevor about the other students she's met. The ones she likes and the ones she doesn't. "There's this one guy, Robert. He's a bit like you, he's really intelligent and sensitive. But he had a rough childhood and kind of burnt out mentally and ended up at the Waterford Hospital for a while. Then he worked as a garbage man but now he's just doing that part-time and going to school. I think you'd like him."

Trevor has work early. While he's sitting on the step to the kitchen, lacing up his sneakers, Rose excuses herself and goes into the bathroom at the other end of the hall. Trevor watches her pull her jeans and underwear down, sit on the toilet, wipe herself, flush, and pull her pants back up. He's too amazed to think to look away. None of this has registered with her as she walks him downstairs for their hug goodnight.

As he holds her, Rose feels something hard in his coat pocket. "Oooh!" She laughs."What's this?"

Trevor pulls out a paperback. *The Tao of Pooh*. "You should read this. I'm finished."

"What is Tao?"

"It's an ancient eastern philosophy. About living simply. I started reading the Tao te Ching first. That's kind of the Taoist bible but I got really bogged down and gave it up 'cause it didn't seem to make much sense for something about simplicity to be so complicated. But then I read this and it all made sense. Winnie the Pooh is the ultimate taoist, the uncarved block. He's got this really simple way of seeing the world so he already is Tao, he doesn't have to..."

She kisses him on the mouth, temporarily halting his torrent of words. Trevor laughs. "Hey! You understand this better than me. Here's me going on and on explaining simplicity to you and you..."

She kisses him again and again until he shuts up but the kissing overtakes them and Trevor hears himself whisper, "My god, I wanna crawl right up inside of you."

Rose takes his hand, pulls him up the stairs, kicks cardboard boxes and clothes aside and they make love on the mattress on her bedroom floor. Trevor's eagerness betrays him too soon. Rose squirms out from under him, "Touch my cunt."

This is a word Trevor can't abide. He never uses it. Can't bring himself to say it. Finds it hard and violent and ugly. But somehow from her mouth it's none of those things. The hard consonants C and T no more harsh than in the word comfort. A soft lingering tone as she emphasizes the UN. As he mulls this over in his mind, emphasis on the UN, he thinks briefly of world peace and chuckles to himself.

He accepts his task with glee. His only serious sexual relationship, while it had lasted several years, had been with a woman who was so Protestant, so white-bread, that the suggestion of anything more adventurous than the missionary position drew from her such a look of distaste that he stopped asking. So this is new territory for Trevor.

His fingers explore the mysteries of folds and fluids, her dark, catacomb world, the novice speleologist mapping her negative space for form and texture and trigger points. She pushes his head down, introducing his tongue to her wetness, and empty spaces in his senses of taste and touch and smell are filled in with her, delicate and bittersweet.

Trevor still has trouble catching Rose at home, even when they've made plans, often driving across town to bang on her downstairs door and driving away downhearted, circling around downtown in the hope of spotting her. Sometimes she'll call from a friend's phone. Ask him to come around. For tea and company and sex. Usually also to ask him for a favour. To drive her somewhere, to lend her some money or help with homework. One time to ask him to borrow his mother's station wagon to pick up a roll of carpet she'd spotted abandoned on the sidewalk. Then help her lay it in her livingroom. Then she decides it's too gross so they have to take it up again. He doesn't care. Anything to see her.

Rose wants to see the new movie about Gandhi so Trevor takes her, then they walk downtown for a coffee. "Thanks for paying. I know you always do..."

"Hey, it's okay. I'm happy to. Is something the matter?"

"Yeah. Fucking Social Services! I thought I could get daycare paid for Melody while I'm in school. Well I can but they tell the student loans and they take it off my grant. Dollar for dollar."

"The government has a vested interest in keeping poor people poor. They have a quota. Maybe we should do a Gandhi, you know, some kind of civil resistance."

"How about this? I can't afford to buy clothes, right? Haven't bought anything new for myself in ages. We should get a bunch of us to march stark naked on the welfare building and occupy it. If they arrest us for indecent exposure we'll say it's our school uniform because it's all we can afford."

Trevor smiles, "It might even be fun!"

"I know Robert would be into it. He'd do anything if I asked him."

Trevor feels his smile tighten down and a familiar ache wash over his stomach. As they walk back toward Rose's place, along Harvey Road, Trevor hangs a moon at the Social Services building. Rose laughs and slaps his ass, "I didn't know you had it in ya!" She flashes her breasts at a darkened window. They run and laugh and bump, hand in hand back to Rose's mattress. They fall asleep there, Trevor's head on Rose's bare belly. He wakes to muffled screams. He holds her and rocks her until her breathing slows. "Tell me. Tell me your dream. It makes it go away."

"No." She turns away.

"It never seems as bad when you say it."

"Don't go home tonight, Trev."

"I'm here. I'm here. What are you afraid of?"

"Everything."

"Tell me."

After a long pause, "I'm in my room, I'm little and cold, but I'm not me, I'm Melody. I'm Melody, and Gary's beating Dad with a stick or something, over and over and over and Mom's just there rolling cigarettes and then I'm alone in the dark."

"Did anything…"

"Just hold me. Just hold me. Don't ask me, I don't want you to know me that well."

A cloudless Sunday and Melody at her grandmother's, Rose calls Trevor. They go for a long drive out of town, walk and run through the autumn woods. Swishing and kicking and throwing crunchy leaves at each other until they get cold. They go back to the car and turn on the heat and drink Kahlua with milk, setting the bottle and cups on the flat dash under the sloping rear window.

Rose twists and wriggles as Trevor unbuttons and tugs off her jeans. She slips off her underwear, "It's a good thing this car is sexy, Trevor, 'cause it sure ain't comfortable!" As he unzips his fly, she grasps his hand, "Hey wait. Me first."

"I know. I know but I'm starting to feel like intercourse is like, I don't know, like second course." His attempt at humour comes out more like whining and he regrets saying anything. What he really feels though is that his brief penetrations are tolerated as encouragement, not for the sake of his feelings, but to keep him around. Because sometimes, he's nearly sure, what she really does need is *him*.

"Think of it as dessert."

What he once thought of as her Tunnel of Love has become her Love Canal, polluted either by his rival or by his own insidious doubts. "Are you sleeping with him?"

"Who?"

"Robert?"

"I told you. We're friends. Anyway, time for appetizers! Come on. You know you love it."

His frustration crumbles with Rose's smile, and despite a lingering stomach ache, his senses are soon overwhelmed with only her. Somewhere in their awkward backseat passion, an errant foot kicks over the bottle and the thick, sticky liquid runs down inside the rear heater duct.

Driving himself home later, Trevor flips on the heater. As he absently savours the smell of her, still pungent on his fingers, the heater floods the car, as it always will now, with the sweet coffee aroma of Kahlua. In the olfactory centre of Trevor's brain, these two scents mingle and form a permanent association, like cotton candy and a perfect day at the fair.

As the dank grey of late fall settles in, most evenings Rose can be found at home, but rarely is it just her and Melody there anymore. Robert is often there now. Trevor doesn't like him. Finds him dull and brutish. Rose's brothers Don and Rick start to come around more, sometimes with girlfriends. There's always beer and dope, which Rose hadn't bothered with so much since she left home.

One night Trevor shows up and Rose greets him with, "What did you bring me?" It hadn't occurred to him that this was one of the few times he'd turned up empty-handed. There was usually something for the apartment or food or wine or some little thing he'd made for her. "Robert brought beer," she says and spends the rest of the evening sitting next to Robert getting loaded. The party is still droning along when Trevor gives Rose a kiss and lets himself out.

Trevor wakes too late for work. Calls and says he's got the flu. Not the first time lately. He goes to The Duck for a coffee. He's staring out the window at the War Memorial, on his third cup, when Rose walks in.

"Hey, Trevor."

"No school today?"

"Geography. Stupid course. I usually cut it."

"Hangover?"

"Yeah, well, you're one to talk, Mr. Working Man. I noticed you polishing off that flask last night."

"Yeah, well... Let me buy you a coffee." What he meant to say was, yeah well, I don't have a little girl to take care of.

He's seen a plastic poster on a bus with a picture of a sad and unkempt little girl. The caption reads, "Are you sure your drinking isn't hurting anyone?" He thinks about stealing it and giving it to Rose but of course he wouldn't do either. He resolves to say something but the opportunity never presents itself. When he's with her he's usually getting drunk himself, trying to keep up. He stays away for days at a time, feeling pathetic for trying to hold on when she's so obviously drifting away. Then he misses her. Wants to save her.

Rose calls and he gets the station wagon, takes her and Melody to cut a tree. They have a great day, down one of their woods roads, throwing snowballs, making snow angels. They put up the tree, string popcorn and cut out paper snowflakes, just the three of them. Then Rose and Trevor tuck Melody into bed and make love and drink hot chocolate.

Christmas Eve Trevor comes by. Rose's brothers are there. Hash smoke and testosterone. Rose's face is cut and bruised. "My God! What happened?"

"Last day of school. We had a party. Kevin Rimmer followed me home. Wanted to come up. I wouldn't let him so he grabs me in the porch."

"Did he, my God, did he rape you?"

"I don't know."

"You don't know?"

"No I don't know, fuck, I can't remember, I think so, maybe, probably, I was drunk."

"Jesus, Rose! You must know!"

"He left and I got in the bath."

"Did he walk you home or—?"

"I couldn't get rid of him, he's a creep. I told you about him."

"Well did you call the police?"

"No."

"Why not?"

"Why would I call the fuckin' cops? Like I said, I was drunk. I'm not even sure if he actually raped me. They'd just hassle me. I been through this before. They're bigger creeps than Kevin Rimmer."

"This has happened before?"

"Trevor. Fuck off. I had a hard day so get off my back will ya?"

"I'm sorry. Oh God, I'm sorry."

"Come in and have a beer or give me a hug or something." She's crying now and lets him hold her briefly, then she breaks away and gets them both a beer.

"I almost forgot. I brought you and Melody presents."

"Oh. Thanks. I can't kiss you, my mouth is too sore." She puts Melody's under the tree and opens hers, a Stevie Nicks album, and puts it on. Robert shows up with a bottle of cognac and she gravitates to him.

The talk between Don and Rick and Robert is all revenge. To go find Rimmer and beat the shit out of him. Kill him if it comes to that. Robert suggests hockey sticks. The brothers agree. They'll go to jail. Fuck it. This is their sister. An eye for an eye...

"...makes the whole world blind," says Trevor to no one in particular.

"Wha?"

Trevor turns to see Don standing behind him. "Oh, uh, Gandhi."

Trevor receives a long blank stare. Then, "Have a draw b'y." Trevor accepts, then finishes his beer and has another, and another, then some cognac. He watches Rose snuggle closer and closer into Robert. He gets up to leave. "I guess I'm gonna go," he says, despondent, "Merry Christmas."

"Hey Trev wait," Rose eases herself off the couch. "I'll walk you out."

As he's putting on his boots in the hall, Rose puts her arms around him, "I'm sorry, Trevor."

Trevor is fighting back tears, "What is he, Mr. Perfect Fuck or what?"

"Trevor, don't. It's nothing to do with that."

"Well what then, 'cause I don't understand?"

"Trevor, I'm crazy about you... but it's like we're from different planets."

"No."

"Yes we are. I can't explain my life to you."

"You won't even try."

"I don't want to have to, Trevor. With Robert it's easy. I don't have to 'cause he's from the same planet as me. Anyway, this place is no good for you Trevor. All this booze and dope, you're making yourself sick. Look at you, you're losing weight, and your ass was skinny enough to begin with."

She's trying to coax a smile out of him when Rick comes out. "Hey Man, it's all set. Two o'clock tomorrow. We meet at J & D's Takeout on the Heights and go for Rimmer."

"Ricky, no!" says Rose, "Tomorrow's fucking Christmas Day!"

"Big fuckin' deal, he won't be expecting us will he? You in, Trev?"

"I'll be there."

"Good." As he heads back to the livingroom, "Bring a hockey stick."

"No sweat."

"Oh, come off it Trevor, this isn't you."

"No. I gotta do this. I can't do anything else for you, but I can do this."

"Trevor, stop it."

"I'm goin' home now. See ya b'ys! Merry Christmas!"

"Trevor..."

Trevor wakes up Christmas morning weeping. He stays in bed past breakfast, then helps his mother prepare supper. He doesn't get dressed until the rest of the family arrive around four-thirty. He takes Anne aside. She promises to check in on Melody from time to time. The Monroe Christmas is a quiet affair.

In the spring the Camaro's chassis gives way. The rear springs protrude into the trunk. Brian says he could weld it but he couldn't guarantee anything because there's nothing much left to weld to. Trevor sells it for parts. While he's waiting for the tow truck, he sits behind the wheel, revs the big engine a few times, then shuts it off. He leaves the heater fan on full and breathes in slow and deep.

Ramona Dearing

Love Bites & Little Spanks

There's a trick to these storms—they come when Lenny is on the road. My husband is a dentist. He has the main office here, and a smaller one in Billy's Cove he goes to every Tuesday. There are two plastic chairs in the waiting area. The door next to one of them opens onto the room with the drill. The other room has a sofa-bed and TV, one of those big braided rugs covering some of the tiles. He stays over when the weather is down. Gracie does too. I can't prove it, because Lenny's only excuse for staying is that the roads are bad. But it's perfect—he won't lie to me. He doesn't have to. You don't take chances in the winter around here. Five people died the week before Christmas, a car and a tractor-trailer. Better to wait it out, that's why Lenny always takes an extra shirt with him.

I see them, the bar in the middle of the bed making them arch like dolphins, the TV on, the smell of burning teeth.

Yesterday I told him he could have her all the time. I meant it as a gift mostly. Also, I wanted him to remember me just long enough to tell me. I need his words, need him to say he is for her.

"What are you doing to me?" That's all he says before he swings for his lunch bag and goes out the door. He slips on ice at the bottom of the driveway and almost falls. He rights himself, stands perfectly still, as if he's reading the graffiti on the hill across the harbour. He turns and nods to Sam next door and clomps away.

Gracie is my cousin. She has a beautiful ass, the kind meant for love bites and little spanks. Her laugh stays with you the way the taste of licorice stays in your mouth. Gracie paints lupins and skeletons. She also does icebergs for the tourists. That's how she gets by, they pay whatever she asks. Greenish white, streaked with purple, big orange splotches for the puffins' feet. She used to sell fishing scenes, the houses and stages all tilting toward the waves. But it's the icebergs people want. She says if she did one right, instead of for money, it would be dark grey against black water. So grey you couldn't really see it, except you'd know it was there.

The top floor of her house and most of the second are closed off in the winter. The rest is always cold. She never gets her wood cut in time to dry properly and her electric heaters are a joke. She's hung moose antlers over her woodshed, they're covered in polka dots. She figures old Nish Collins down the road will hang her cat in revenge one day.

We were laughing drunk, putting on lipstick in the bathroom of the Star of the Sea hall when I told her. Kissing in his car, wriggling. That was a few years ago.

"You?" she said. "You?"

Lenny was in Quebec City at a dentists' convention. Every time I woke up, Herbert's hand was still on my hip. I decided I would tell Lenny as soon as he got back. But when I went to St. John's to get him at the airport he told me he'd been thinking we should get a dog, he'd do all the work.

Herbert phoned once after that, and I went over in the afternoon. We didn't say hello, just took our clothes off in the living room. After, he said we could never be together again. He told me he had a cavity and didn't want Lenny's drill to slip.

Then serious: "It's not me you're after. The two of you go walking, and everyone stops to watch you pass. The whole fucking town stares, but you never notice."

"What's this then?" I say. He shakes his head, sad. We kiss, one little breath after another.

When it blows, this place twitches and hums. Downstairs is not so bad, though the wind sucks at the stove damper like a tongue on a chalky peppermint. Upstairs, the bathroom fan clunks and the window in the front bedroom whines against the frame, even with rags pushed into the crack. There are strange easy moments between gusts, until another one pushes at the house. The outside walls move then, just a little. The water in the toilet sloshes back and forth.

I usually pour a couple of rums to mute the din. Some nights I reach under the bed and pull out the fiddle Lenny's Uncle Albert left him. I let it shriek until my elbow aches. Or I pluck out a lullaby the wind will never hear.

I've tried to learn as much as I can from Wilf Stokes. He comes for a visit sometimes, has one small nip before he'll play. His fingers mash the strings.

"It's like this," he says, but I can never see what he's doing. He listens with his eyes closed and doesn't say anything when I'm finished. One time he said, "You'll be good enough one of these days."

I tutor his granddaughter, Jacinta, in exchange. Wilf says the more French she knows, the easier it will be for her to get work on the mainland. He says this as if Jacinta's leaving has already been arranged, although she still has another year of school. She's hopeless, but sweet. Every time we meet, she tells me I have pretty hair. A couple of times her father has asked me to phone in an order for his hardware store to a company in

Quebec. Plastic flowers for graves, Gore-Tex jackets, skidoo parts.

I want to know when Gracie stopped thinking Lenny was boring. She used to roll her eyes when he talked, or lean back and let her head rest on the top of the chair.

He hangs the tea-towel over the oven door and sits at the table. I know he is comparing us. Our gumption, our tantrums. Me in a nightgown, her. The light in the kitchen is too bright. The dough sticking to my hands makes my skin itch. If I could, I'd make snowflakes all day long, each one lacy, cut with very sharp sewing-scissors. The secret to a good one is to leave only tiny wisps of paper holding it together. It should be mostly air.

"Play for me," he says.

The smell of the bread is strong even in the living room. I stand by the window, don't notice how the frost has blocked the window until after I put the fiddle down. Lenny is in the kitchen. I hear the scrape of the oven rack, the soft thuds as he turns the bread out of the pans to cool. He stays in the kitchen until after I fall asleep.

Lenny's hands are too clean. He wears rubber gloves to do the dishes, and heavy cloth ones in the garden. He rubs his hands with lemon after chopping garlic. Lenny wants to be soothing, inoffensive as he pries open his patients' mouths and leans in. He says there is no way to erase the fear, even if the drill didn't make that noise. But his touch is warm. I know some of the wariness leaves as his fingers push down on their cheeks.

Coca-Cola is stripping them down to the gums, he says, eating through their teeth like dry rot. At the strip mall last week he saw a baby with pop in its bottle. He went over and spoke to the mother.

"Right you are," the woman said, "but from what I understand, you've got some bad habits of your own to mind."

When he told me about it, he stared at the clock and said he was sorry. I heard later it was Edith Butt he'd been talking to.

I floss every day. Sometimes I leave the bathroom door open so he'll hear the sound of the thread going pick-pick through my teeth. He doesn't care, he says my breath is good, but I've always thought you should bend a little, show someone you can move in their element with ease.

I phone Gracie. We go to the Pot-Luck, order eggrolls and hamburgers for lunch.

She says, "He's a lot better than I expected."

I know Gracie too well, I don't say anything.

"Do you want him back?" she says after Stella pours water in our glasses.

I stay quiet. Gracie picks up my hand. Her fingers jerk and jump. When I look back up to her face, she starts to giggle. I laugh too. A tiny piece of chewed burger lands on her cheek, but she ignores it. There's a steady buzzing, a low beep-beep outside. The lift bridge going up. I brush off her cheek. She leans forward across the table and talks softly.

"How about a three-way?" She wiggles her eyebrows.

"Before bingo or after?" I ask, and now we're bouncing our feet on the floor and Gracie says, "Buy me a beer before I piss my pants."

Last night Lenny stayed away. I dreamt his uncle Albert died all over again. A bunch of us stood around the casket, and every so often someone would say, "But he just got a job last week. He just got a job." And that made all of us cry, waves and waves of tears.

Lenny phones in the afternoon.

"I won't be around much for a while."

"Oh," I say. And that's it.

Sometimes I wonder what the odds are of shuffling a deck of cards and having them come out in perfect order, the way they are in a brand new pack.

Marge's kitchen has a red kettle, red canisters, even red plastic measuring spoons hung on hooks. Cream yellow walls. She pushes a plate of date squares over to me.

I'm laughing, telling her at least if I ever need a root canal, it won't cost anything. Telling her I expect Gracie to plant my garden for me and feel so guilty she'll weed it for me too.

Marge says, "That's right honey, you just let it all out. You just keep going, honey, and work it out of you. You just let it come up."

The red and white boxes on her gingham tablecloth hurt my eyes.

"Just heave it out of you," she says.

When I walk home, the kids are shooting down the hill by the cemetery on their magic carpets. They try to run back to the top but their feet kick out and sometimes they slide all the way back down on their backs, the bright plastic scooting ahead of them.

Herbert gets up from the couch to get me another beer, and the floor shakes under his feet. He lives in a thirty-five-foot trailer. The glass I'm drinking out of has a thumbprint on it. He sits at the other end of the couch, staring at the TV. It's on, but the volume's turned down.

"How can I do you?" he says. A car drives into a jungle sunset. We sit there. Then he says, "If it takes the sting away, he didn't get a new woman. He's got the exact same woman. You and Gracie just traded places is all."

"Asshole."

"Exactly what she would have said." He's still grinning as I put my boots on. "But remember it's Liz I'm wild for."

We chose the house for its colour. A yellow that almost passes into orange. The house is the shape of a tea crate on its end. Out the windows of what used to be the parlour, you can see over the steel wall built to keep the waves from spilling against the houses when there's weather. The wall is rusting, the rust bleeds through the snow that's been pasted on by the wind. On a notepad I write, *I do not want to remember this time.* I rip out the page, fold it into a chunky wad and hide it at the back of my underwear drawer.

"I wasn't going to sleep with him," I tell Marge the next morning, "I wasn't going to sleep with him ever again. I just went there."

"You straighten up," Marge says. "You dipped your toes. Now you're complaining they're muddy."

"No," Gracie says. "You can't." Her nostrils flare wide. She's slouched forward with her breasts pushed up under her arms. "Does Lenny know?"

I want to get pregnant. I want my belly to jump away from my ribs, to flower crazily. If it's a boy, I'll get a sailor suit with baggy knickers made for him.

"I know I'm old," I tell Gracie.

"Are you asking for him back?"

"People will just keep saying what they've been saying, only they'll have some more to say."

I want to cross my eyes and stick out my tongue. I want to go tobogganing. I am bursting, restless.

"Have you been careful?" she says.

"Have you?"

"I'm throwing up a little bit," she says.

It's getting dark out and her kitchen floor is cold. I make her some tea.

Lenny gives me a puppy for Christmas. "Cuter than I ever was," he says. The dog cries when there's a gale. He trembles against me and licks my hand.

Lenny takes down the moose antlers hanging above Gracie's shed. She's working on a painting, she's got it in a room on the second floor. She locks the door when she's done for the day. Her stomach is pointy.

We compare Sobeys stories. She's sure she hears people hissing at her, soft, under-the-breath hisses. I get the *you poor dear* looks.

I have four suitcases and a case of partridgeberry jam in the back of the car. The dog's chin bumps the edge of the window, paws scrabbling the seat. A job lined up in St. John's, at least for a few months. A translation contract for the government.

I'm leaving the house the way it is for now—blankets on the bed, the curtains up, placemats on the kitchen table. I give my plants to Gracie. She holds my hand and her tears wet down the fuzz on the baby's head. Ellen howls until she feels a nipple on her cheek.

"I'm the one who should be going," Gracie says.

The way she says it, it's not an apology. Lenny stands with his hands in his pockets. "At least show her your painting before she goes."

She shakes her head, and lowers it over the baby. When I pull out of the drive I feel Gracie's eyes on me, the way you feel an old woman watching you from behind a lace curtain.

"So you'll be leaving us for a while," Wilf Stokes says. Even though I told him a couple of weeks ago. He pats the top of the car. "Now don't come back from the city with an earring in your nose or any of that." I smile. He looks up, lets his head tilt and roll as if he's examining each cloud. "Looks like snow. You'll come right back if it gets messy, won't you." He hands me a bottle of moose.

"You stay steady," I say. The violin is in the back seat. I have a feeling I won't play it again for a long time. When I get to the bridge, it's up. I put the car in park and wait. The dog barks after a couple of minutes.

Medina Stacey

The Smell of Holiness

*I*f we could escape our memories, where would we be–in some white land of ice or snow or vapour; some place free of the taste of gumdrops, the skin of tulips, the smell of sardines. We would not walk for we would have forgotten the ground. Life would not be a good enough name for this place.

Our memories are blanched onto our skins like those stamps on old suitcases that you only see in the movies, like the one George Bailey constantly packs but never uses because he just can't leave home. Paris in blue letters–that young boy you shared a Coke with when you were ten, London–the song your mother always sang when she washed dishes, New York–hopscotch in the April mud, Tanzania–the taste of happiness.

Half the time people just buy those stickers at the drugstore and stick them on. Who did you ever know who went to Tanzania. But it sounds nice doesn't it?

Perhaps its white and warm and quiet there. Perhaps the purple fruit makes everyone forget the day before and the footsteps that trail behind them on the sand. Perhaps they don't count the steps. Perhaps they don't look for the mysterious second set of prints that lets us believe we're not alone. Perhaps the women wear long white cotton dresses and the tinkle of their jewellery against their skin lets them know what time it is. Perhaps they're sad and poor and cold like us, with shoe boxes stuffed with old ticket stubs—admit one, and pictures of people who've long forgotten them, stuffed under their beds.

I remember a woman who bought a book with money she had for shampoo. A book with a beautiful cover of a woman sitting at a piano, with her head on her hand looking at a window. Although she in not playing we somehow know that she can. She sits in a square of cool blue and looks toward red. Marjorie bought this book the September her daughter started school; she put it beside the picture of her parents on the coffee table and talked to the three of them the way some people talk to holy pictures. Other people noticed the book and picked it up the way you would a beautiful child. They asked her what it was about and if the plot was exciting and what happens to the beautiful woman. She was surprised, she never intended to read the book, just look at the picture.

But she could not say this, so she told them the story of a woman who marries the wrong man and falls into despair and is never able to play again, she tells them the story of a woman who goes on journeys to faraway places in search of treasures—ancient texts, Chinese vases, misplaced paintings, and she finds them for other people who pay her a salary. She tells them of a woman who kills herself because she loves her family so much and they have not known suffering. She tells them of a woman who forgets that she's alive. She tells everyone a different story and they marvel at the beautiful book. She does not say these are my stories, these are my women and I have made them dance and cry and scream. She puts the book back on the coffee table and drinks tea and saves to buy more shampoo.

The old man tried to get the waitress's attention, but she kept looking away, distracted by more orders for burgers and fish and roast beef sandwiches. She tries to remember what everyone wants and wishes the old man and his thirty-seven cents would go somewhere else for a cup of tea. She shouts to Marjorie in the kitchen that her kid is here and gives the girl half a Coke. The little girl sits at the end of the counter waiting for her mother to send out leftover french fries. She does not notice the old man until he is directly in front of her. He leans into the space where her plate should be.

"How are ye, t'day, child?" he talks at her, through clenched teeth, "gettin a mug up, are ye?" She blinks. "Look here, look here, fasten yer eyes on this awful beautiful ting"—he puts both hands into one of his pants pockets and tries to get hold of what he's looking for. "Look here," he repeats and she watches his hand move about in his pocket, waiting for the magic trick.

"See this, look here, girlie"— a crumpled piece of coloured paper, " here it be," he spreads the paper out, patting down the edges. "She was only a child herself, I daresay twelve or eleven. From France she was, do you know where that be to?" She shakes her head. He squints his eyes shut as if he is conjuring up a map in his mind. "Never mind," he says and sweeps the idea off the paper with the back of his hand.

He dutifully moves the paper when the waitress brings the little girl's french fries, and he smiles at her, hoping for a cup of tea, but she refuses to look him or the little girl in the face. She thinks they're both beggars and a waste of her precious lunch-rush chance for tips.

"It was a long time ago, yea. She had fourteen brothers and sisters, and God himself spoke to her, through the Blessed Virgin." He is holding a coupon for a St. Teresa nightlight. He moves his mouth as if he were smiling and uses his finger to keep the little girl's attention directed at the cartoon-like picture of the young saint. "She went right up into heaven, right up," he waves his arms in the direction of the flourescent lights. The child mechanically eats her french fries, careful not to get ketchup on the old man's coat.

"What's yer name, anyhow. I'll order ye one. I'm havin' em sent in from the States. A dozen I'm gettin' for all me nieces. Ye write yer name and where ye lives down and I'll bring herself to ye, one day soon." The girl blinks and licks the ketchup off her finger. "Can't ye write? Sher yer a big enuf girl for that, aint ya?" Her eyes move across his face, scanning for signs of humour or authority. This man just looks silly. She takes the coupon and writes her name in big loopy letters. "That's the girl, yer a good little one, somethin' like the saint herself. I'll bring her to ye, as soon as they gets here from the States." He put the coupon back in his pocket. He pats her on the head and she notices how he smells like the old soup her mother brings home, that's been left in the fridge too long. "Do you want a chip?" she asks and holds up a long, overcooked, greasy slice of potato.

In the preface it says that the woman who wrote the book died before she could finish it. Someone else had picked out the title and cover. The writer had put stones in her pockets and walked into the river, not a warm river either. Marjorie holds the book in her hands, and wishes she had the courage to start the story.

But the story started a long time ago. Once in a room by the sea, a woman sat at table, near a window, and travelled the world, took many lovers, sang, knit, took tea, had babies, rode horses, roasted beef, planted tulips, danced at balls, had her hair done and watched the clouds move beyond the trees in her garden. She had written the words, she had made them real.

They had changed her name. The woman used to talk to her as she wrote, softly, she'd say, "Now Annie, what will become of you today? Are you well, Annie? Do you like you're new man, Annie?" She used to be called Annie but someone had erased it and given her a fancy name, a name that no real person would be called.

September had brought them all to the old house, full of newspapers, some at least two years old, painted unsigned pictures, gathering dust in every corner, convincing him that Annie was rich. It never occurred to him that she might have painted them herself. Once she had told him that she was the messiah. He laughed at her and sang her a silly song about the sea. Now he was not so sure.

Annie liked to watch snowflakes fall, liked the smell of sheets slept on by someone she loved, liked buttered toast at three in the morning. There was no wasteland in Annie, no space for lost memories, she kept everything neatly, labelled and stacked in cupboards, on top of shelves and under beds.

She liked them best when they fell straight down, no wind to rustle the places already settled. She didn't like draughts. Still cold or soft heat, but not strange winds that blew rotten leaves through her head, winds that shook dogberries from the trees to be squashed by some boy on his way to school. Later his mother will scold him for the stains on his trousers. Annie sees all these things. Her eyes are large and brown and deep like soup that heals the sick.

To reveal the world would mean that someone would have to draw back the curtain–someone's hand must be raised and touch the lace, wool, cotton, bars, and let the light in. Then the sunshine would flood the kitchen, making it warm, and the sun would shine directly on that spot, she thinks, pointing her finger and willing it to happen. It would wax the square patch of floor, tickle the arm of the chair pushed back from the piano, flick the towel hanging too far away from the sink and dance through her hair like fireflies. She stands on the spot and raises her arms over her head. No one opens the curtains, so the floor stays cold under her feet. Where has the gentle woman gone?

He is still asleep, she dislikes sleep, it keeps her from gathering things. She has gathered music and recipes and friends in basements and attic rooms, pictures of old men on street corners, and women with babies and idiots drooling, waiting for the bus. She gathers and waits for the day when words will make these pictures real. She makes tea and waits and sings a song of the sea. And waits. A snip of sunshine sneaks through the curtain, she hopes that if she tries hard enough the light will break through and she'll see the picture clearly then and the pain behind her head will go away, but no hand raises the hard cover.

To forgive would be a famous lie. Betrayal is wet and damp, and lasts as long as spring with snow in June. In the dream he kissed her and wrapped her in the orange blanket. They lie peacefully side by side. But this is her dream and sometimes it isn't him who saves her—sometimes it's the man in the record store, sometimes the man who sells newspapers, sometimes the dark man who drinks his tea from a saucer at the café. She knows that there are no facts, nothing to support all the dreams—she writes a note 'you have kissed me a poison that is sweet and then taken my heart and crumpled it like a page with too many misspellings.' She leaves it by his bed.

In the dream he sees her swimming, jumping in and out like a dolphin, she is laughing and showing off for him. Then she walks towards him and the water, white and shiny as it slides over her flesh, won't leave and it turns into fingers, grabbing and pulling her legs back under and he can't move, she is screaming and sinking below the surface. He can't move. He wakes up in the dark and listens for the screams he never heard. There is a note on his pillow.

She sinks into a pool of dark water and all the hands reach out to touch her and she sees them all smiling beyond the surface. The sky beyond them is red. She is asleep, upright in the chair beside the piano, waiting for someone to open the curtain and call her by her name.

Marjorie hates soup. Hates the texture, the way everything is thrown in together. She doesn't like bits of carrot and potato and rice all floating on some pale broth with too little meat. She is hungry, but she doesn't want this goddamn soup. Perhaps she'd get a bath before her daughter came home, but she worried about the cost of the hot water and she still didn't have any shampoo. If her boss was a more decent man he'd let her take the leftovers home, but he never offered and she knew by the look in his eyes that if she asked, he'd keep account and one day expect to be paid back. What to eat. There was bologna, but she had to keep that for her daughter's supper. She hadn't been able to steal any ketchup packets from the restaurant and she knew the child wasn't going to want the bologna without it. She looked out the window and wished she had a cigarette.

She wished she had some coffee, she wished she had something to eat, she wished for anything. She looked at the lines on her hands, her daughter called her skin crusty. She traced the longest line to the tip of her finger, this meant a very long life. Her father had said she had artistic hands, that she'd be a painter or a piano player, but she had never learned, never tried. Now it was too late. The skin on the back of her hands was bubbly with scars from the deep-fat fryer. The fat bubbles up so high sometimes, it strikes her face. They don't like to change it too often, the boss says it's a waste of money. So she spends a half an hour every day picking through the grease, painstakingly removing the charred remains of potatoes and chicken wings from the vat. This is not how she thought she would live. She is glad her father only exists in this picture. She watches the boys on the side of the building across from her window throwing rocks at the streetlight and wonders why her daughter hasn't come home yet.

He was standing under the sign that led off the main road into the square of buildings where she lived. When she saw him she knew he was waiting for her.

"How ya, girlie. I got somethin' to show ye." He moved from side to side, his hands buried in his pockets. She had forgotten all about St. Teresa. She waited for him to take his hands out of his pockets and give it to her.

"Come on with me, now, and we'll go and see this wonderful thing. It's not so far, ye'll see, it's somethin' awful nice." He moves his head up and down, slowly raising his eyebrows like the face of a muppet, she thinks.

The boys have broken the streetlight and stand around kicking rocks and sharing a cigarette. These boys will never do anything, Marjorie thinks, half of them will end up in jail before they are twenty. But they all dream of big cars and exotic places. They pack their suitcases every night and fly off to places that only exist on movie sets. They move in a world that is large and open and only exists before you turn twenty. They wait for youth to be over, for their big break, for the scam of the week that will make them all rich. They will take the yellow brick road to Toronto and they know exactly what they'll get when they get there.

They have a plan and no intentions of stopping until they're full. This place will be nothing more than a memory, a word abbreviated on the tag of their suitcases. The impatience to move is born in them, it runs backwards from the illusions of the old into the young, the hope of something better shadows their lives like an exotic fruit dangling purple and golden, without knowledge they are sure it will taste sweet.

. . .

He pushes open the large heavy door. She has never been inside a church before. The colours are so beautiful and it smells really clean and like something else she's never smelt before. She asks the old man what it is and he mumbles something, and she thinks he says, "It's the smell of holiness." He shows her St. Teresa smiling down from the window, her eyes not quite open.

She eats the soup without bread and lays the bologna in the oven and waits. Such a nice day for the playground, the grass is just starting to turn green. She hopes her daughter won't get her clothes dirty, she has nothing else cleaned for tomorrow. She puts her feet up on the coffee table and the book falls on the floor, the pages open, spread as if someone had just left off reading. She picks it up and looks at the woman, half turned away from her, staring out her own window. She flicks the pages and settles in. This is where she belongs. There is nowhere else to go.

    She lays her hands on the words as if they could raise themselves to touch her.

Annie was flooded by a square of light, she sat peeling an orange, her bare legs now warmed by the rush of light. She sucked at the core of the orange to catch all the juice before it ran down over her chin. Her face was open and beautiful like a table spread with white linen. She turned to smile at the other woman...

Beth Ryan

Family Business

My aunts all look the same. Long noses, big horsey mouths, and a mop of curly hair that is always threatening to break free of a French roll. There are four of them, each born not a year after the last one. No wonder old Nan O'Neill's face is always screwed up, like she had sat on a tack or banged her bony shin off the gnarly leg of the dining room table.

Each of the aunts is named Mary something—Mary Margaret, Mary Elizabeth, Mary Patricia and Mary Agnes. But the O'Neills call them Peggy, Betty, Patsy and Aggie. After Nan had babies for four years running, she and Pop took a little rest. But by the time Aggie went to kindergarten at Mercy Convent, Nan finally came through with the boy child. They stuck him with the name John Francis William James Michael O'Neill but they call him Mick. Most of the time, I call him Daddy but sometimes I like to call him Mick too, just for fun. It bugs my mother though. She tells me not be so "precious" so I do it when she's not in the room.

Nan O'Neill loves Mick more than life itself, I figure. He always gets first pick of the chocolates when a new box of Pot of Gold is opened at Christmas time. Nan smiles at him from across the room, from her big velvet throne next to the fireplace, and she says "Mickey, give your mother a hand with these, will you, darling?" My mother usually leaves the room at this point and if you're near her, you can hear the sound she makes—a pretending-to-throw-up sound. Mick hops up from his chair and darts across the carpet to get at the chocolates. That's why there is never a maraschino cherry or a filbert cluster left for anyone else. But he makes it up to me. There is always a full box of maraschino cherries in my stocking every year. I eat them all before Christmas dinner and sometimes I really do throw up. I just can't stop myself—it's a tradition.

Mick met my mother when he was at the university for a semester. She was taking history and Latin and literature and making the honour roll. She was president of the Debating Society and played the violin in a quartet. Mick was there because Nan O'Neill said so. He was a boy and it was his job to make the O'Neills proud by being the first in the family to walk across the stage in his cap and gown. But Mick spent a lot of time in the canteen, smoking cigarettes, drinking Pepsi and charming the girls, my mother says. He never went to classes. In fact, one of his professors posted a sign in the main lobby with Mick's picture on it and the words "Have you seen this man?"

"That stupid old codger thought he was funny," Mick grumbles when my mother tells this story.

"It *was* funny," my mother usually says. "We got a grand laugh out of it."

When my mother says "we," she means her and Ted Hogan, her fiancé at the time. He was brilliant and witty, she says, with a little sniff in Mick's direction.

"Come on, Eleanor," my father says and chucks my mother under the chin when she talks about Ted. "Ted was a boring old fart who thought he was a big deal because he'd been in the war."

My mother always has the same response.

"Ted is a doctor and the president of the Knights of Columbus and a respected member of our community."

"And he'd put you to sleep in a second," says Mick, laughing and pretending to snore at the same time.

I like to hear stories about how my parents got married and, of course, I get completely different versions from the two of them. I quiz my father about it when we are alone in the car. He usually takes me for a drive on Sundays if he gets up before lunch time. He comes into the living room with my coat flung over his arm and jingles his car keys at me.

"Care to go bouncing over the potholes, Miss O'Neill?" he says, bowing grandly in my direction.

Our Sunday drives take us in one of two directions. Some days, it's time for a "bay run." My father calls everything that exists outside the city limits of St. John's "the bay." We drive to Torbay or Middle Cove or Portugal Cove. That's often how I get my best stories. My father's tongue loosens up when he has a steering wheel in his hand. When Mick is feeling less ambitious, we stick to the familiar streets of town. We head out Monkstown Road and down over Prescott Street and make a few passes of Duckworth and Water Streets, waving to people out for their afternoon walks. Then, we retire to Willie's tavern for what my father calls "afternoon refreshments."

Willie is not supposed to be open on Sundays so we go around to the back lane and sneak in that way. It's a special arrangement for Willie's special friends. When we come in through the storage room, Willie always pretends to be surprised.

"Well, hello old man! What brings you by on this fine Sunday afternoon? And who is the charming young lady with you?" he asks, as if Mick has never spent a whole Sunday afternoon here.

"William, it is a pleasure to see you," Mick says, shaking Willie's hand and slapping him on the shoulder. "This is my lovely daughter, Meg. We are just out for a Sunday drive."

"Is that so?" Willie says, and looks at me with a big smile. "Well, as you know, Mick, we're closed today. But can I offer you a beverage? On the house, of course."

He and my father exchange a couple of exaggerated winks and we take a seat at the bar. For me, a beverage means a weird kind of lemonade that Jeanette, the barmaid, whips up for me. And for Mick, it means whiskey—neat. We usually sit there for a couple of hours and I get some good stories out of my father this way. But it's hard to know if they're any bit true.

The way Mick tells it, his romance with my mother was like a big Hollywood movie starring Rita Hayworth, shot in colour, with lots of dance scenes. Ted Hogan was out of town one weekend at a Catholic men's retreat and Eleanor went to a dance at the college auditorium with some of her girlfriends. They were chattering and giggling and casting long glances at the guys sitting nearby. But Eleanor just sat there in a dress as dark and dusky blue as a berry, with one long leg crossed over the other, and watched the action on the dance floor.

"The thing about your mother is that she loved to dance," Mick tells me as if he was letting out a dark secret. "But old Ted was a bumbler on the dance floor so she never got a chance to strut her stuff."

On this particular night, Mick asked Eleanor to dance and twirled her around the floor, letting her dip and spin until she was dizzy. By the end of the evening, they were partners for an impromptu dance contest, which they won handily, Mick adds with a wink.

"By then, she was hooked. There was no going back to Ted the Dead," he says, hopping out of his chair and walking around like a zombie. He does this all the time but it still makes me snort lemonade through my nose.

Eleanor broke off her engagement to Ted a few months later and started going with Mick, a move that set the tongues a-wagging in town. People would look at them with narrowed eyes, as if they were hoping to peer into their heads and figure out what was going on between them. Their classmates came to the conclusion that Mick and Eleanor were a very odd match.

"Not that your mother cared," Mick tells me, with a hint of pride. "She couldn't be bothered with what they all thought of her. Your mother was a bit of a mystery to the crowd at the university. They didn't know what to make of her."

There was no doubt that my mother was different from everyone else her age. For starters, she lived alone in a cottage on the top of the hill on Carpasian Road. She owned it outright. Her father died when she was five and left the property to her. Her mother had married again and had two little boys—"horrible little hellions"—so Eleanor cleared out of there as soon as she was allowed. The cottage was a lovely spot with a fancy front room and a studio where she could practise her violin and set up her easel for her watercolours. She would heat up tins of soup for her supper and make toast in the little kitchen. And in the afternoons, she would pour endless cups of tea for the girls and they'd sit in the front room and talk and listen to the radio.

Eleanor's father also saw fit to leave her an inheritance. Nice of him, I figure. My mother wasn't rich but she was "comfortable," as she calls it. She had enough money to pay for her tuition at the university and for her violin lessons and art classes. And when she wanted a new piece of sheet music, she could just walk into Hutton's Music Store and tell the clerk to put it on her bill. And he would say "Of course, Miss Tobin. That will be just fine." All the bills went to the lawyer, who paid them without comment every month. She did not have to explain herself to anyone.

"But everything changed when I married your father," my mother tells me, and she sounds a bit sad then. I guess she really misses her music lessons.

Eleanor married Mick on a Sunday in August. A warm, silvery fog lingered over the wedding party for most of the afternoon, keeping the sun away. But it never rained, which was a blessing. As it was, Eleanor's fine hair was already frizzy from the damp air. Her friend, Doris, tried to control it with pins and sprays but it floated over her head, puffy and cloud-like.

"Good thing you've got this hat," Doris said. "Otherwise, you'd look a fright."

"Aren't you a comfort!" Eleanor said, in her snippiest tone.

My mother didn't want to look like every other bride she knew, decked out in white gowns, with layers of white net shrouding their heads. Anyway, she says white does nothing for her fair skin and reddish hair. In the end, she wore a long dress of silvery blue with a wide-brimmed, floppy hat to match. The wedding ensemble came from the Model Shop downtown and Eleanor thought it looked quite smart.

"Will there be any men at the reception?" Doris asked, while she fussed over Eleanor's hat.

"If there are, you'll have to fight Mick's sisters for them."

The wedding reception turned out to be quite the party. Mick and his friends kept things going for hours, drinking and singing, their arms thrown around one another's shoulders, their faces red and their eyes teary. Eleanor danced with Mick and his father, and each male guest in turn, whirling around the dance floor in her elegant gown, looking every bit the queen. Mick made several toasts to his new bride, the love of his life, the most gorgeous woman to ever set foot on the college campus. But each one made a little less sense than the last. It was almost three o'clock in the morning when Mick picked up Eleanor and swung her through the door of the cottage, knocking her head on the door frame.

After the wedding, Pop O'Neill decided it was time for Mick to be a man and earn a living for his family. It was finally time for him to join the family business.

"I will see you down at the store on Monday morning at eight o'clock," Pop tells Mick.

But Nan intervenes on Mick's behalf.

"Now, Francis, the boy has just gotten married. Give him a chance to get settled in," she says to Pop.

Pop tries to argue but it's useless. He gives in and says Mick can come in on Tuesday. Nan counters with a week from Monday and walks out of the room. The deal is done.

As the oldest, Aunt Peggy was the first of the crowd to go to work at the family's clothing store. They sell overcoats and tweed jackets and salt and pepper caps to all the fine gentlemen in St. John's. After a couple of weeks on the job, it was clear to Pop that Peggy is a natural at the art of retail sales.

"It is a joy to see that girl sell a coat," he says, with genuine admiration. Pop is not too good with the customers himself. He's stiff and awkward and can't find much to say to people. So he has respect for someone who can cajole money out of people's wallets and make them feel happy about it at the same time.

But Peggy is modest about her success. She credits it to forty per cent knowledge of the goods and sixty per cent knowledge of human nature.

"I just show the men what looks good on them and if they look good, they feel good," she says, as if it was the easiest thing on earth.

On her thirty-fifth birthday, without a husband in sight, Peggy marks her seventeenth anniversary at the store. Under her direction, the O'Neills have done well. Three years before, Pop bought the building next door and expanded the store, adding sections for children's and ladies' clothes. Pop decides to give

Aunt Peggy a reward for her loyalty and the permanent toothy smile she has for the customers. Everyone goes down to the harbour to await its arrival.

It's a surprise, says Nan when the aunts press her for details on the gift. She snaps her mouth shut like a change purse and says nothing else. A huge cargo ship is docked at one of the finger piers and dozens of people are clustered on the wharf, looking up at the ship's deck in anticipation. I poke my mother every so often to suggest another possibility.

"Maybe it's a horse!" I speculate. "Or a husband!"

She looks down at me and gives me the darkest of her renowned dark looks.

"Really, Meg, is there any need to talk about your Aunt Peggy like that?" she asks and I know I am not expected to respond to that question.

My father is chatting with everything that moves on the dock. He buzzes around like his shoes are on fire. By this time, he has been working at the store for almost five years. But it's not like anyone would have noticed, my mother says. Mick doesn't actually spend a whole lot of time in the store. When I leave for school, he is usually still in bed. When I get home, he's rarely there. If he comes home in time for supper, he'll come in to the living room and listen to me play the piano for a few minutes. I try to play something bright and upbeat to keep his attention, to keep him in the room. But I know it hasn't worked when he gets up and kisses me on the cheek, blowing his sweet whisky breath into my face. After that, it takes only a few minutes before he and my mother are arguing in the kitchen.

"Look, something's coming off the boat," Aunt Aggie calls out to the rest of the family.

I look around for Mick to let him know the surprise is coming. But he's nowhere to be seen. Finally, I catch a glimpse of him standing off to the side, next to someone's truck. He's talking to Jeanette, the barmaid at Willie's tavern. She is eighteen, not old enough to work there. But she can handle the customers like nobody else, Willie says proudly, as if he had invented her himself. I like Jeanette. She's kind of saucy and funny, and she swears more than most boys I know. A rough bucket of bolts, my mother would call her. When my father and Willie launch into baseball talk at the tavern, I get Jeanette to teach me card games. She's a real pro. The last time we were there, she showed me how to play blackjack. She deals like an expert, slaps the cards on the bar with authority. When I lose a hand, she laughs. She laughs a lot, with her mouth wide open and her head tossed back.

But Jeanette is not laughing now. She is pointing at my father, her finger stabbing the air below his nose. Mick is wearing the strangest expression on his face. I slip past my mother and snake through the crowd to get closer to the truck. Jeanette's voice is bouncing up and down, hitting high notes I've never heard from her before. By the time I get near the truck, I can hear that she is crying, sniffling as she keeps on talking.

"I don't care what you tell Eleanor," I hear her say in a soft muffled voice that I barely recognize.

"I'll work it out," Mick says and he takes her hand, pats it like it is a kitten or something.

"You better do something. I don't have much time," Jeanette says, and starts fishing through her pockets for a tissue.

Behind me, people have started clapping their hands. I look up at the ship's crane hovering over the dock, a huge wooden box dangling from its claws. I look back at my father and Jeanette. He is holding her arm just above the elbow. I step out from around the back of the truck and Jeanette sees me first.

"Daddy, the surprise is coming off the boat right now," I say and my voice is very calm.

Jeanette smiles at me and blows her nose. Mick lets go of her arm and turns around.

"Right you are, darling," he says and starts walking in my direction. He turns back to Jeanette. "I guess I'll see you later at Willie's."

The box is slowly moving towards the dock, inches at a time. I can see Aunt Peggy with her hands clutched together in front of her chest, as if she's about to sing with the Mercy Convent Glee Club. Pop is beaming at her. His face looks like it could bust open. When the box finally touches the ground, a couple of men rush toward it with hammers in their hands. They start prying the nails off and pulling the end off the gigantic box. It is big enough for a half dozen people to stand up inside. Mick stands behind me, drumming his fingers on my shoulders in time to some tune he's whistling. My mother is a few feet away, watching us both.

The wooden square finally comes free of the box and the men pull it away. Pop steps forward and offers a hand to Peggy. They walk together and peer into the box. She turns around to the crowd and screeches, her hands over her mouth.

"It's a car! It's a brand-new Buick!" she says and does a little dance before she throws her arms around Pop and plants a big wet kiss on his cheek.

The crowd is quiet as Aunt Peggy stands in front of the car, her mouth open and her hands fluttering. Then, my father starts clapping, a loud hollow sound echoing out of his cupped hands.

"Bravo, Peggy! No one deserves it as much as you," he calls to her, and the rest of the people start applauding and whistling.

My mother looks at Mick curiously, as if she's never seen him before.

The next morning, my mother comes into the living room and finds me lying on my belly on the carpet, reading a book. I'm supposed to be practising the piano but she doesn't seem to care. Instead, she sits on the piano bench and crosses her legs, one long, elegant leg over the other, the pointy toe of her shiny brown pump hovering near my face.

"How would you like to go on a trip to the Boston States? Just me and you! We'll get on the boat a week from Monday."

This gets my attention. The Boston States are all we ever hear about from the aunts. Peggy and Patsy went there once to visit some of their girlfriends from Mercy Convent who had gone to get jobs. They lived in Cambridge and worked in the bank. Aunt Patsy gushed about the clothes they wore, smart suits nipped in at the waist and dresses splashed with polka dots, topped off with matching hats. Peggy talked mostly about the excellent business opportunities that existed there, especially in the gentlemen's apparel trade. But that just made Patsy giggle and snort.

"I don't think it was the apparel that caught her eye! I think it was all the fine gentlemen!" she said, one hand over her mouth to catch the laughter.

"That is not the case," Peggy shot back, all puffed up like a hen. "I am only interested in ways to improve the family business."

Patsy said there were so many people from Newfoundland living in Cambridge that it almost felt like home. They even had dances especially for the expatriates. Ever since that trip, she's been trying to convince Pop that she should go down there and get a job but he says he needs her at the store too.

My mother had never been very keen on the idea of the Boston States. She always muttered that Patsy was just a bit too flighty for a woman her age. What was all the fuss about, she'd ask, looking around for someone to give her an answer. There was nothing in Boston that we couldn't have here in St. John's.

"Well, what do you think?" my mother says, and her foot starts tapping on the hardwood floor.

"Sure," I say. "How long would we go for?"
"As long as we want."

Mark Ferguson

Stan and Edward

*E*aster. The room was still except for their breathing, the baby with a cold, snuffling at her breast. There were men working and machines thumping in the distance, down at the dockyard. The loneliness of the clanging sounds, of that bustle way off in the distance. For all of them the holiday had already ended. It was over. The cool air poured in the window, across him. Arlene's hand drifted back across her and into his face and Edward kissed it lightly, but it was a false kiss. Her eyes were closed, a strand of her hair was falling across her eyes. He didn't know what to do now. For about an hour he had felt very far from her. When they were walking home from the restaurant—they were so tired—he had begun feeling it, suddenly, a loss, a drop in his love, a change in intensity. It was a scary feeling. Pushing the baby up the hill, Arlene two or three steps behind, slower, he was falling out of love, and when they came home and lay down, the feeling was still there, growing even, that distance.

He hated the west end. He hated it now, he wanted to move away. He had for weeks, for months. Since he was twenty for Christ's sake. The cat was mewing in the kitchen. He couldn't move from the bed. He hated the neighbours. Fucking lawyer George, that morning screaming again—screaming at his wife for what seemed hours. Sunday morning for Christ's sake. It was exhausting. He didn't know what to do. Finally they had had to leave the house. He hated the cat. Shut up, you stupid fucking cat. Edward's wife almost crying, her hands across her ears. He got the baby ready in the front hall. He heard the boy come into the situation, the son yelling at the father. The boy's yelling abruptly cut off, the yelling stilled for an instant, the heavy thump into their wall. Muriel, the wife, her loud crying for the first time, her cries rising, louder and louder and the front door slamming and a glimpse of the boy on the sidewalk, quickly, his head down. A minute later, George went out too, in the same direction—up the hill.

First Stan and Emily were up against the front of a house, leaning on an old-style verandah. They were thirteen. April day, the weather kept changing from gray to blue and then gray again and then it would snow for a few minutes, big flakes and then it would stop. They had dirty newspaper delivery bags, they had them off their shoulders, and they were using them to cushion their bodies from the wall. The house fronted onto a steep street, going down drastically to the Waterford River, and directly across from the house was Victoria Park, also rushing down to Water Street. The two children gazed steadily into the park, a ball field just opposite, a flat bit. The girl who was tall and slender and had blond straight hair took her bag from behind her at one point and dropped it at her feet.

"Frigging useless," the boy was saying, "completely friggin' useless. Fucking old *Telegram*."

"Stan, it's all you got—"

He said he didn't care, he was tired of lugging papers. She said she would help him with his route, they'd get them both done faster that way. There were still newspapers in the bags. They had been talking for a long while and it was funny how close they stood, very close side by side, and how they seemed like an old couple, so comfortable with one another even though they were so young.

"Emily, it's ok for now, it's not winter, you should see the winter—"

"I wouldn't care you know —"

He started to tell her about what it was like going up Sudbury on a shitty winter afternoon. How everything got soaked and freezing, you, your bag, the papers, how your customers complained and complained.

Emily said; "We'd get them done —"

"And all for a few bucks a week, eleven cents a paper, twenty-two on Saturdays—it's useless." He hung his head, turned his face down, he was a tall thin boy, pointy features, skin pulled tight on his face.

"It's better than nothing." They were dressed thinly too, clothes not fit for the cold.

"What I'm saying, Emily, is it is not much better, you know? Not much better than nothing."

"Your dad won't give you anything —"

"Course he won't—course he won't. I didn't say he would."

"And neither'd my mum —"

They needed the money. They both smoked and they had already started talking about saving money for their futures.

"Fuck." He spit. Quick, little nervous spit.

"Stan." He wouldn't look at her.

He said: "We could get money —"

"How?"

"I don't know, Jesus—steal it." He pushed himself off the wall and started across the street, bringing the bag. She picked hers up and followed. He went down over the sidewalk onto a grassy slope and he stood there awhile, the bag hanging at his side, just barely off the ground. She came up beside him and they contemplated the park.

"Ground's wet." she said.

"Yes. Shit." He was looking away from her, distracted or pretending to be.

"Let's sit on them." She was looking at him. "Let's just sit on them." She tapped his arm, getting him to pay attention. "Stan, why don't we sit on them?"

"Sure, ok, yeah." She dropped her bag first, dropped it brazenly, with a flourish. It skidded down the hill a little, and came to a stop. Then she took the bag dangling from his elbow and dropped it to one side of the other. She took a step down and tucked her legs under her as she sat upon the bags. Stan joined her then, and as he was sitting he was taking two cigarettes out of a plastic case and handing her one and they lit them up and they started to smoke.

"This is some shitty old fucking park, piece of crap." said Stan.

"It's not that bad." They were making themselves comfortable on the bags.

"The pool's gone, the swings are shit. It's all for kids. Man, in some other place, a real place, a real city, there'd be a great big park, it'd be huge, not this crappy little park." She wasn't listening—she was staring off across into the open sky, blue at that moment, she was thinking about another place, some other place and not here. Suddenly for no reason, she cuddled toward Stan, she leaned up into him, continuing to smoke. It brought him up short. He stopped talking, stopped complaining.

He started thinking about the night before, walking home from Emily's up Leslie Street. He remembered a car idling on the hill, outside a house. It was cold and as he went past it he could see dash lights on inside and the dark form of a person in the passenger seat. He could hear piano music coming from the car, weird music, a kind of music he had never heard before, and he almost stopped for a moment to listen. The warm music coming from the warm car. Halfway up the hill he started humming a tune, an aimless tune, a bit like the piano, started thinking about Emily.

Kissing her, just that while before, outside, on the little walk beside her house, out of the light, away from the kitchen window. Feeling her through her yellow winter coat, pressing feverishly against her. The kissing very intense, very serious. Just before they had had a smoke and Emily was chewing some gum now, some grape gum, so her mother wouldn't suspect. He was thinking of how she took it out of her mouth to kiss him, stuck it behind her on the fence for retrieval. Then how her hand came up to his face, moved from his cheek and then around through his hair and behind his head, as she became more intent on the kissing, their tongues coming into each others' mouths then, the cold disappearing from the dark night. Why kissing was invented. Maybe. Then the way her face and his own face moved when they were kissing and he kissed harder and harder, and how their faces were moving so violently, faces in a commotion in the heavy kiss.

The boy was humming that song he heard off the radio. He sang:
>I'm putting together a picture
>of what happened...

Then the chorus:
>My baby loves me, my baby loves me, my baby loves me.

He thought: Anyone could write a song.

· · ·

When Arlene woke up from the nap, the baby was still asleep. Edward was up, he had been too tired to sleep. She came into the living room. She said she wanted to move. There were deep circles of exhaustion under her eyes. She had had enough. The incident that morning had done it. She was afraid that George's screaming next door would start to affect their baby. She was frightened of George. She couldn't stand seeing his two kids all the time. Her eyes filled with tears. She sat down beside Edward on their sagging couch. He put an arm clumsily around her shoulders and she cried for a moment, leaning against his shoulder. She wanted to do something about George. She didn't know what. She said they should move away and then report him. She wanted him stopped. Edward kept genuinely agreeing with her until she asked: "What are we going to do?"

"We can't afford to move right now."

"I can't stand much more."

"He'd murder us in court. He'd probably sue the fuck out of us. We wouldn't even get to court. He'd threaten us into submission." They'd gone over this before. They had no idea how the legal system worked in these cases. Who got charged, who took who to court. They kept meaning to find out, call legal aid or something, anonymously, ask about the rights of it. They both had the vague sense that they were doing something illegal by not reporting what was going on. Edward said: "He gave it to him today. Poor little frigger."

"Goddamn it." Stan was making it. He was really going, it was sunny up ahead. The roadway was shimmering, like a mirage. It had been raining and cold earlier. Now it was sunny and colder and the wind had picked up and it was right in his face. But he felt good, not cold. He could see ahead and it seemed there was someone coming forward from the distance to meet him, and that person was shimmering too. He was moving towards Stan and it seemed each step the person took was like he was walking in water up to his waist and having to push his way through it, like coming through a bog or a swamp or on marshy ground. Something slow and steady, like he was floating a little somehow as he walked.

He was hungry before but that hunger was gone. He had rushed out of the house without anything–no breakfast, no smokes. Before he had been weak, really weak, Christ, tired, and every step was an effort. He wished so much he'd had a smoke. Now the hunger had become a tingling; he was light, his legs were light, his whole body felt light, he could make time, he could cover the ground. He wondered: did he look the same way to the person who was approaching him? Did he? Was he like a mirage to the guy?

Glancing to the right, there he was still, his father, still keeping up, staying close. George. He was right tight to him, walking calmly, evenly, pacing, dogging him. He didn't think George could have kept this up, he was pretty amazed at George—his staying power. His father on the other side of the road. He didn't care anymore about George there though. The sun was bright when it was out, super bright, blinding. Harsh cold light. The water was freezing on the road again, cars were slipping a bit when they hit the wet patches, slushy places where little streams seeped over the roads from all the rain. He was cold when he thought about it, the thin coat was wet through and even walking fast couldn't stop the chill—he thought he might go into that Tim Horton's by the road that went to the airport—fuck George then. If George came in there, fuck George then. He wouldn't be responsible for what happened.

Now he was up in the east end, behind the Confederation Building. He'd been walking for over an hour, maybe two. At the beginning, up through his neighbourhood, he had hardly been thinking about what had happened, about his father, what he'd done. It had been a long steady climb up out of the west end. He had kept cutting east, going across the hills, on the lanes and then across Sudbury through the park.

His mind had been full of other things, big songs, big loud music he kept singing to himself silently. George was behind him about fifty yards, but he, Stan, never took notice, never gave him the one sign he knew he was there, fuck George. Fuck fuck fuck George. There had been colours in his head, bright colours, explosions, faraway places, nothing normal, sensational lights, warmth and activity, people, not the people he knew, shouting but not that shouting earlier. Merry-go-rounds or something, ferris wheels, shit like that. Nighttime, daytime, parks, pies, contests, music. A girl.

All things he dreamed before but never thought about, things he'd done but couldn't remember. Was it TV, was it shows he'd seen, or movies he'd seen over to Emily's?

He'd called her in the middle of his father going nuts that morning, he'd called Emily. Stan had been staying calm, wound up though, really wound up. He could still hear his Dad, George, downstairs yelling. Dad screaming and screaming himself hoarse. His mother murmuring now and then. His father yelling over her. Julie crying quietly in her room, and Emily, fuck—great—Emily not answering, Emily not home, and not her mom either and not her stupid little sister, no one, no answer. The perfect day to choose to go out somewhere stupid, probably her mother, her mother's idea, perfect.

Stan had seen it coming the night before. George waited till Sunday morning, nothing normal about Dad. Fucking wait for Sunday morning to go nuts again. No one else in their right fucking minds would wait for a Sunday morning to start blasting, to go into fucking deadly mode, Jesus H Christ Dad. Stan was thinking about the neighbours—both sides hearing it all again, Dad again, Sunday morning, everyone's houses so quiet.

Now it was Sunday afternoon and they were walking. George his father, walking behind, now across the road, keeping up. What did he want? Stan got a great urge to stop right there, a great huge urge to stop right there and turn and look at him across the road, and just go mad, just let it rip, you fucking son of a bitch you go back, you go home, you fuck off, you son of a whore, you whore's cunt, you piece of shit, you go fuck yourself twenty-seven times on a fucking stake, up your fucking fucking arse—you worthless piece of shit.

His jaw was clenching, he could almost feel his body moving, big broad obscene gestures. A finger up, pelvis thrusting, and throwing-up motions, and madly waving his arms and then bellowing, screaming. He felt his teeth grinding in his head, his hands in fists, wanting to beat him, beat him down and kill him. Beat him and kill him, finish the pig right off—for all the shouting and shouting at his mother—"For Christ's sake Dad leave her alone you bastard, you cunt, you fucking cunt—"

Suddenly this fury had come upon him and for the first time pain behind the eyes—tears maybe. His throat locked and burned. Before it had all been a daze, the bright lights, wheels turning, gigantic wheels. He had shut off the panic, but now it was back.

How stupid things entered his mind as he walked—stupid stupid things. The woman at 23 Sudbury, the old woman, Mrs. Cowan, how she was nice to him, how she never was nothing but nice to him and always paid and never complained, and gave him tips regularly, nothing big, but regular tips. Her house smelled good and it was quiet, but nice quiet, like there was something calm and kind there. This woman's daughter had been there lots of times and paid him and smiled at him and tipped him better than her mom, and thanked him for doing a good job for her mom. He could see this daughter was a kind woman too and he figured the whole frigging family was like this, really nice and so kind. They were warm generous people and they could afford to pay him. He had never seen the old woman's husband, never an old man around, he probably died or something. Left a bundle, lots of these old guys round here had bundles all over the place, buried in their frigging basements for all he knew. So Mrs. Cowan could probably afford it and she didn't mind, she didn't deny him a little extra every other week or so.

He had crossed over the river at Pippy Park a few minutes before. He'd seen the dark water pouring out of the pond. It was high with the rain and he thought about that kid they always talked about, that little kid who got drowned years and years ago, who got pulled into the brook that came down through Victoria Park before the city covered it over and had the pool taken out.

He couldn't remember that river. Christ, he'd never even seen it. There were certain spots, storm sewers, you could hear the water rushing underground. That kid that got drowned, he popped into Stan's head, no reason, just there. He thought about the stories about him he'd heard for years. Getting sucked down under Water Street—down through this grate and into the sewer and drowned. They pulled his body out by the Waterford. Man, that kid was old and dead before Stan was born but everyone was still talking about him—how come? How come they were still talking about that poor kid, like it was last week or yesterday or last year?

About an hour before, there was one place by Prince of Wales Arena where George had come right up beside him. George hadn't said anything or done anything or looked at him. Stan hadn't said anything or looked at him either. He wasn't ignoring him on purpose. He just couldn't, like he was suddenly numb and empty and had nothing to say to him. Nothing to give him good or bad, nothing at all to encourage him in any way. He was calm. Not waiting to be comforted or to get walloped again, or dragged back down the road, back home. He wasn't even considering George as existing just then. His father was completely out of his thinking right at that moment.

George never said anything either, or gestured or put an arm out or made a face, a grimace, or said "Stan, Stan, come on now son, come on now, let's go home, let's go back, let's let bygones be bygones, son—" No. Hadn't said that, just walked along beside, grim and quiet. For about a block and then at Linscott Street, Stan had crossed over the road again and George hadn't crossed with him.

He'd started thinking about Emily at about this time, before he had crossed over and away from George again. Emily and her nice brown shirt, the shimmery, satiny shirt that opened a bit at the waist. Sometimes when she stretched he could see her belly button, her flat smooth belly. The shirt was a strange brown, with grey in it or silver, a dusky colour. It wasn't a strong or bright colour, but there was something good about that colour for him. He liked her in that, how it made him feel when she wore it with her jeans, how pretty she looked.

One time when they had just started going out, they were kissing in the house. Her mom had left and they were kissing and he put his hand there, on her stomach, beneath her shirt. He felt her warm smooth skin, her beautiful stomach under his hand. She gave a little shudder, just a little one, when he touched her stomach and she kissed him a little harder then for a minute. She didn't open her eyes or try to stop it or move his hand, she just kept kissing him. There was a hockey game on.

Stan looked up again for the person approaching. He didn't know if it was a man or a woman or a kid, but when he looked up they were gone. He couldn't figure where they'd gone. It was gray again, a patch of gray, and it felt like it might snow. How had the clouds come again so fast? The person approaching hadn't crossed to the other side. There was no one only George, and only the woods on his side. He was puzzled for a bit. Then he shrugged because he figured they must have gone into the woods. There were paths all through the park.

It was weird but it felt lonely that he'd never met the person who had been coming towards him. Not knowing which way they had gone made it seem worse somehow. He wanted to know where they had gone into the woods, but he had no idea. He almost turned and called out to George, without thinking, "Hey Dad, Dad—where'd they go?—where'd that guy go?" As if suddenly things were fine, were normal again, as though the morning had never happened or the night before. It was as though they had all sat as usual and just watched the game, his sister cuddled into his father. He realized he wasn't thinking badly of his father all of a sudden—that was so strange, very strange. The rage had let go of him. As if Stan might stop walking away now or slow down walking and then stop. Pause a moment on the side of the road and then turn around and start back. Get home and call Emily. Get home and call her and he saw his mother there then too, in his head—how was she now? Trying to picture her home. She must be worried. The papers. His papers. The fucking *Telegram*. Shit. Maybe Emily'd tried to do them without him. She'd do that, cover for him.

The week before, Edward was filling out an Employment Insurance form. It was a series of affronts. "Have you ever attempted or are you now attempting to knowingly defraud the Canadian government? Yes or No." Oh definitely yes to that one, about one hundred times. Lying and defrauding all the way.

"Are you taking a leave of absence?" Yes, heading off to Europe for about six months. Mainly the south of France, the Riviera.

Then, down at the coffee stand, the counter girl was half pretty and half surly and refused to heat a raisin scone. Edward could feel himself flush, become slightly fawning—even obsequious. He thought that maybe she could pick up on his vulnerability—unemployed, with a kid, few prospects, already nearly out of money. He asked her for butter. Perhaps she caught his frown as she handed him the Becel. Fucking margarine, he was thinking to himself, not butter, fucking margarine. He was counting the change in his wallet, realizing he didn't have the money for the bun. He was short twelve cents. Twelve cents. Before he could stop himself—he was hungry—he quickly pawed the scone, so she couldn't return it to the display case.

"Maggot," she said low, harsh, then quickly—"why don't you get a job?" His mouth dropped, his eyes widened.

He recovered: "Look—I can pay you the difference next time—"

"Don't come back here if you can't pay—"

Christ. How fucking insane. It was always the people with the shit jobs on the periphery of the powerful white collar types that went for you. Christ, she was just a counter girl in the bottom of the Unemployment Office. There was something cruel and angry in these people: working their guts out for minimum wage and you meekly passing through, you on EI, just as shitty, but they turn on you, pour on the abuse. All the cheerful guys with the suits and their frigging potbellies. They worked upstairs, pulling down forty or fifty thousand easy–and grinding you down with their patronising smiles, their suspicion, their scepticism. Then heaving down here, chatting up counter girls like this every day, free and easy, laughing. For Christ's sake. They had you.

Not only that—there was foreign matter in the scone, a goddamned black hair, baked right into the thing. He looked around: the basement cafeteria was populated mainly by people like him, the underemployed, the poor. To be seen in this basement, to drink coffee there, it tainted you. Ruined you. You were a leper. There was a security guard at the next table, talking to a seated man and woman. The man was called Barry.

"Still nothing Barry?" The guard was smiling down kindly at the couple, but Edward sensed—or maybe he was just imagining it—no, he was sure he could hear the self-satisfied tone in the voice of the guard.

"Still—no, nuh. Nothing Frank."

"Jeese Barry. That's a tough one."

"Yes sir, that's it."

"Christ yer fifty years old, aren't you?"

"Now, no—no, no, sir, I'm in my forties."

The night before. Saturday night. When he got in Stan was aware right away how quiet it was, very still. No sound, no TV, no music, no radio. Lights were on, except in the living room, kitchen all lit up, living room off to the side, no lights but he could see his father, George, sitting very still in his chair, smoking a cigarette, looking straight ahead at nothing. His mother was missing. She must have gone upstairs and Julie too, though it was early for a Saturday, she usually watched the game with Stan and George, but the game wasn't even turned on. The kitchen was clean, spotless, as usual. The dinner dishes were all in the dishwasher—he could hear it ticking—it had just finished. Everything else shiny and in place. Newspapers on top of the fridge. Ashtrays all on the sill, spotless. Floor spotless. Shiny. Quiet.

His father's voice too was quiet, controlled. He asked Stan where he'd been. Stan kept moving through the kitchen, headed for the stairs up to his room. He told him he'd been out with Frankie and them. A lie.

"You're late son."

"Dad—It's Saturday—"

"You're late for a Saturday, Stan." So now Stan had to stop to converse, to turn back to his father's voice from around the corner. Flat and quiet.

"Sorry Dad—"

"Jesus Stan—you're always late—"

"Dad—"

"Don't 'Dad' me—"

"I'm not that late—"

"Don't Dad me—I've had just about enough of this—from all of you—" His father stopped listening at that instant. His father started something else then: a private conversation with himself. Or it was with his family, but they weren't actually there. Invisible stand-ins for his mother and himself and his sister. They were there standing before his father and perhaps some other man—a judge—a person George was appealing to, saying "Give me goddamn strength to deal with this crowd—Jesus."

His voice vehement but calm: "Give me the goddamned jesus strength and patience to deal with this goddamned fucking crowd. Your mother Stan, your mother is crazy. She's doing her goddamned level best to drive me crazy." Stan said nothing, stood quiet not even able to see his father, just the voice around the corner. He could smell the cigarette smoke, wanting to light up himself. "She walked out around this evening Stan, walked right out around." Stan had no idea what he was talking about.

"She had plenty of room—plenty of room—she could have passed between your sister and me, but no—she chose to walk out around your sister's chair—not come near me—what have I done? What have I done to offend her?"

"Dad—I've got my Tely accounts—" But George heard nothing now.

"The witch. What's she up to? Is she trying to drive me insane? Cause she's succeeding—she's succeeding in a big way. She claimed, son, she claimed it was nothing, just happened that way, just happened to swing out wide around the chair instead of going between—just an accident."

"That's too bad Dad—I'm gonna go upstairs now—"

"Accident. I'll show her accident. Shit."

"Good enough Dad—"

"Stan—for god's sake—quit interrupting your father–"

"Dad—I gotta go."

Stan!" The voice loud and harsh. "Shut up while your father is trying to tell you something—I'm trying to tell you—I'm trying to warn you against your mother. She's a mean, nasty and hard-hearted woman and I wouldn't doubt but that she bears malice towards me—and perhaps you too son, you never know—"

"Dad—I doubt it."

"Stan—you're a fool to doubt that—a fool—you don't know her like I know her son—"

"Dad—" Stan hated this part. His father trying to turn him against his mother. "Dad I gotta go do my accounts, I'm tired—"

"You're in on this with her aren't you Stan? Aren't you? She's got you hasn't she—"

"Dad—that's crazy—"

"Oh crazy now am I?" Now plain anger in his father's voice.

"No—"

"Stan—spare me. Stan, don't try to pull that shitty old moth-eaten piece of wool over my eyes son. You make me sick.

Get out of my sight. Get out of here, go up to her then—join her and your sister, their little schemings. You little bastard."

Stan stood very still. Not moving, just listening, waiting. He could hear the dishwasher, the buzz of their electric clock. He had to wait, give his father the opportunity to start up again. There was a certain length of time, then he could quietly turn and go.

"I said go, you worthless little shit—"

Stan did. Moving quickly through the door to the stairwell and up the carpeted stairs, two at a time, not running, just long strides, he could feel the muscles in his calves pulling, and when he went by his sister's room, heard her radio turned down very low, tinny AM station, a pop song he could not make out. He went straight to his own room and he closed the door quickly. He stayed sitting on his bed for a length of time, a good while, without a light on. He was looking out the window onto the backyard. The tree there was a dark shape in the night. The neighbours behind, across the two yards, their house too was dark. He turned the bedside lamp on and then very quickly off again, lay down on top of the bed clothes with his own clothes still on. He put his hands behind his head and waited for sleep.

Edward was out with his son, Tom, in their little front patch. It was almost dark. Tom was so small on the frozen ground reaching for a little plastic shovel. He made his noises. Edward glanced up and he saw Stan trudging down the street toward them. It had been hours since the incident that morning. First Stan tearing out, followed by a hurrying George.

Stan turned in the walkway to his house. Edward said, "Hey Stan."

"Hello Mr. Moores."

"You all right?" This brought Stan up and he turned and looked down across the little wire fence erected between their front walks. He kept edging towards his house and he kept his eyes down.

"Fine sir, fine." he said.

"Tom, Tom!" he looked back at his son, "Tom, say hi to Stan!"

"Hi Tom, hi Tommy boy, how you doing?" Stan managed a cheerful voice. Tom looked up for a moment, but he did not really see Stan who was on the front stair by then. The cheerful voice cut Edward. The hopeless lie of the cheerfulness, the will required to summon it.

"Ok Stan. Good night now. See ya tomorrow." Edward managing a smile, but his eyes stinging, little tears.

"Yeah Mr. Moores. Good night," and Stan went back in through the door, betraying nothing. Light from inside his house spilled out as he did.

Edward stepped to his son, bent down and scooped him up in his arms. He turned to his own house. As they came through the door, Arlene was sitting at the back of the house, in the kitchen. First she had a hopeful smile as he came towards her holding out Tom for her to take—but Edward was weeping quietly, not to upset his son. She took the baby upstairs, saying, "Daddy's upset now. Daddy's sad, Tom—" Edward at the table, face buried in his hands, shook with it.

Michael Jordan Jones

Monster Ovulation

I.

That Thursday night Corinne taught the yoga class because the regular instructor, her husband David, was out of town again. He had probably been called away to conduct a workshop at his sect's retreat house in the Laurentians but possibly for business reasons. David sold a line of vitamin pills to health food stores from St. Jérome to Trois Rivières and lately as far away as Québec City.

Corinne was tall, strong, flexible as hell, and usually quite shy. To my surprise she led the session with humour and panache, a tough little class full of hip stretches and repeated standing postures. Imitating her husband's technique she made a point of touching everybody, adjusting our positions just so, running her long fingers up and down our spines to check for proper alignment.

I had a big crush on Corinne. After several months of classes together we had begun to meet at out of the way cafés along the Main and on the Plateau, places her husband never frequented. More recently we had spent a number of evenings together at a Greek bar drinking and kibitzing with my artist and dope-dealer friends. I was dealing a little myself in those days, hash and grass only though, nothing stronger. Afterwards, sometimes quite late, I would walk her to the corner of Fairmount and St. Laurent, nearly home, and I had noted with some excitement that our parting embraces had intensified.

At our little *tête à têtes* I pieced together her story. Born in the Gaspé, moved to Montreal. Her father ran off when she was four never to be seen again though there were letters from Florida which may have contained money. Her mother drank, a lot. At age six Corinne's chores included doing the laundry in the dingy basement of the building they lived in, and on one occasion she crawled onto the row of warm dryers and fell asleep. Her mother found her there, saw the clothes still wet in the washer, and, not untypically, beat her.

At fifteen she was pregnant. After grisly rows with her mother she left home, got an abortion, worked in a restaurant and finished school. At nineteen she was knocked up again in Mexico by either Ramón or Luís. She returned to Montreal to have the baby without telling either of them. She had not spoken to her mother in four years and wasn't about to.

She gave birth, lived on social assistance, started yoga and met David who had just started teaching. They fell in love and were married Shaktipatananda-style by the Swami himself who had a special affection for David, an earnest disciple passionately committed to his spiritual growth.

David was tall, wire-thin, high-strung. He had bright grey malamute eyes and long, clean, feminine hair that he tied back while teaching and let loose after class. Although not symmetrically handsome he was endowed with a more useful trait, a powerful pheremonal quality that only some men have, a scent of sorts that inexplicably stimulated women. As my buddy Alan used to say, the dogs on the Main knew when David was about.

Corinne and David lived in a large flat on St. Dominique with her (not his) eight-year-old daughter Tamara and for about a year David's mother who had come to live with them after her husband (not David's father) had been killed in a bizarre accident, crushed by a city bus that had lost its brakes near the foot of Mount Royal.

Corinne was an artist, or wanted to be. She had studied sculpture at St. Anne de Bellevue but had yet to actually make any saleable art except for a bust, a man's head, that was part of a clothing store window display on Laurier. I saw it, it wasn't bad.

She saw something in me but I was not sure what. I was from Newfoundland, in Montreal looking for casual work as an actor, taking a course in stagecraft, keeping a journal that I hoped some day to make into a novel. I did not stand out in the crowd, shall we say. I was living on unemployment insurance, mailing my cards home and having the cheques sent to me. I had been married but was now separated. It had not been a pleasant split. I had fallen for someone else and though it had not lasted long the damage had been done. You know how it is.

I had a son, now legally in his mother's custody, the same age as Corinne's daughter. I missed him a fair bit and sent him a letter every few days, or once a week at least. He wrote me back occasionally, when his mother put him up to it, and I would show the letters to Corinne who took the same interest in my personal history as I did in hers. I did not tell her about my modest trade in illicit substances, however, fearing she wouldn't approve. She was the budding guru's wife, after all.

Don't get me wrong, she wasn't perfectly pure. She drank with purpose, keeping pace with me and my friends at the Skala, and she smoked, too, though not around David. She had special breath mints that she sucked on with a whistling sound as I walked her up Avenue du Parc toward the neighbourhood we both lived in.

One day we were at a little place on Rachel having a *café au lait dans un bol* and I saw a look of admiration (maybe love) in her eyes. I asked her, "Would David be jealous that you are here with me?" She shrugged and pursed her mouth in that French way, letting out a little puff of air.

"I doubt it," she said. *"David est au-dessus de tout ça."* He was above all that and besides, she told me, smiling, she was the faithful type. I wondered about that.

The truth was I was intensely curious about her sex life with David. How did the Swami's disciples do it, I wondered, what esoteric techniques did they employ? The suspicion that I could never measure up to David's yogic lovemaking had made me shy, reluctant to pursue her too vigorously. If I asked she might say yes, you see, and then the truth would be known.

"Well, you seem satisfied, at least," is all I could say, still hoping she might volunteer some information.

She smiled inscrutably. "I am not easy, sometimes, in that department," she said.

"Not easy to satisfy, you mean?" She nodded and then began to tell me about herself, how she loved to make love, more than most women, she thought, and about certain times of the month she was inordinately desirous.

Naively I asked, "What times of the month?"

"Certain days on which if a man came to visit me I never would open the door unless I had the chain hooked," she said.

"Like you would. So?"

"I would tell the man he could not come in unless he wanted to have sex with me, that's all. He might come in, he might not. But I felt...*obligée de l'avertir, au moins.*"

"Warn him, why?"

"I could not be sure that I would be able to control myself, *tu comprends?*"

"Oh. Yes, I see."

"Monster ovulations, that's what I called them." Her eyes were bright with mirth. "This was before David, of course," she added, laughing boisterously, in part I was sure at the sight of my astonished face.

I had never heard of such things, but I decided to investigate. From that day on I started to take note of when she was menstruating, obvious in yoga classes when women on their period would not perform certain *asanas*, mainly the inverted postures, and I would mark my calendar and observe her in the weeks that followed, rationalizing it as a kind of research into the human condition.

II.

After the yoga class I took my time, dressing slowly, waiting while she collected money from students, watching her pull her jeans over the black tights she wore in class. Together we walked onto St. Laurent. It was a warm fall night and the sky still had light in it.

"Let's buy some wine and go to my place," I said as if I had just thought of it but in fact I had waited weeks to say this. She shrugged, again in that French way, raising her eyebrows and protruding her lower lip, keeping me in suspense, and then said, "*Pourquoi pas?*"

She knew I was subletting an apartment across the street just south of the yoga studio but she had never seen it. Armed with dépanneur wine we mounted three stories to the spacious loft I had lucked into, the abode of a *cinéaste* named Léa who had left for India to shoot a film about Tibetan refugees and who was to interview the Dalai Lama himself.

She made a little circle of the apartment, one big space except for the bathroom. She looked intently at the pictures on the walls—Buddhist monks, spiked Himalayan peaks, zealous young backpackers in Kathmandu, snaps Léa had taken years before—then glided like a snow lioness toward the kitchen table lit blue and cool by the last soft light through the west window behind me.

"I can't stay long," she advised. I was pulling the tight, dry cork. Because of her daughter, school the next day. I poured the cheap wine into Léa's elegant glasses, telling Corinne how good she looked tonight, how graceful she was. That was the word that best described her. She smiled and hoisted her wine.

She was feeling good. She had taught a great class. But more, she told me, she had recently seen the light about a few things. "For a long time I was lost in pettiness and hatred," she allowed. "I was poor, I was living *au jour le jour*, hand to mouth you would say. I was angry, I guess. But not anymore. I choose to love people, now. You have to let go of the negativity, I tell myself. It's work to survive in this life."

I asked her if her husband had contributed to her insight. "Yes, David has helped," she said. "The yoga makes me strong and I am not wondering where the next meal is coming from." Then to my surprise she appeared uncomfortable, almost distressed, and her eyes went moist.

"I am not...*sharing* myself," she murmured.

I asked her what she meant.

"David has been busy a lot," she said, lifting her sad eyes. "I am spending most of my free time with you."

We talked then about the yoga. There were people in the class who didn't exert themselves the way she and I did, we observed. Corinne and I always made maximum effort, exhausting ourselves fully, and we had to acknowledge our superiority in this respect.

After an hour she got up to leave. She had to make a lunch for Tamara. She needed her beauty sleep. She was worried that she was not spending enough time on her art.

She stood for a moment looking at me. I became aware that I was staring at her, and she at me. I have been accused of using my eyes on women, and maybe I was doing this. In any case she approached me and leaned down for a kiss, the usual goodbye kiss I took it to be. I placed my hands lightly on her waist. She did not withdraw but held me around the neck and placed the side of her face, her cheek and ear, against mine, then kissed me again, this time on the neck, softly. I reached my arms around her and drew her down so that she sat on my lap.

She put her arms around me and we stayed like that, embracing, for perhaps a full minute. My heart began to pound with an unusual knocking sound and I could hear hers racing, too. Then without looking at me again she stood up and moved quickly away. I followed her to the door but she was gone before I got there.

From somewhere on the stairs she shouted, "*Salut!*"

I understood. I had been counting the days.

III.

She called at noon. Tamara was home sick but she had gotten some work done. "I miss you, isn't that funny?" she said.

Within the hour she appeared at the door. Her brown eyes burned. She wore a shimmering red jacket of some new synthetic material. She refused the fresh coffee I had poured. "I can't stay. I just want to touch your face and look into your eyes and..." She paused. "*Peut-être...*"

"*Peut-être* what?" I asked.

"*Peut-être t'embrasser,*" she said, removing her jacket. She pulled a chair from the table and set it so our knees were touching, then grabbed my face with both hands and drew me forward so that we were kissing with open lips, really for the first time. Right away she leaned away and sat with her straight yoga spine barely touching the back of the square wooden chair and said, "*C'est tout.*" That's it. No more.

She put on a serious expression and even though I knew she was only teasing me I felt a big rush of disappointment. She could obviously see it on my face because she said, laughing, "*Oh, le pauvre p'tit pitou!*" and immediately leaned forward for some much more serious kisses. Our tongues touched and I felt a surge of energy. *This, finally.*

I pushed her back, stood up, took her hand and tugged at her as if wanting to take her somewhere. She knew where. *"Non, Michel,"* she said. I yanked harder. She resisted, would not stand up. But she would kiss me sitting down, that much had been proven, so down I went. We sat very straight and placed our hands low on each other's hips and started again, freely, no restrictions. I could see she was turned on. I pulled her to her feet once more and although she put on a little show of resisting she let me lead her across the room to the thick futon under the open east window that looked out onto the Main. Across the street I could see the lurid orange and blue sign, *Shaktipatananda Yoga Centre.*

We knelt on the futon and kissed and then sat back on our heels and grinned at each other like demented dolphins. We put our hands on each other's shoulders and stayed at arm's length until we could endure it no more, then came together and fell over onto the bed. She was into it now. I helped her peel off her sweater and then unfastened the top button of her jeans and ran my hand over the bare skin of her hip onto her ass then up onto the skin of her strong back. Oh Christ.

She was making little sounds, holding my face the better to aim her mouth and tongue at me. I undid her zipper and reached my hands down into her jeans to dislodge them slightly. Between kisses she said again, very softly, *"Non, non,"* though by this time I was not taking it literally, knowing she didn't mean it.

I slowed down a bit, though, all the same. I did not want to hurry her. I kissed her slowly, little pecks, lips brushing, nothing kisses, waiting for my chance to get on with it.

Not that I was actively thinking these things. They were half-thoughts flitting through my mind without lodging there. Sex is like driving a car or chopping wood, you can think whatever you want and still do the job.

And I knew that Corinne was most likely having her own reflexive preoccupations, subconsciously recalling past loves, making the inevitable comparisons. There would be images of David, or Ramón, or Luís, or maybe someone else entirely.

I knelt up and she let me pull her jeans off by the cuffs and she uttered a tiny mournful sigh of resignation as I stripped off her underwear and both our shirts just as the sun broke free and streamed in on our bodies from high over the Swami's headquarters across the street.

We lay quiet and naked for a time, basking in the warm light and in the anticipation, adjusting, considering the risks. That moment, you know it. On the wall beyond her was a Tibetan *thangka* depicting a male deity of stern visage peering at us from over the shoulder of his naked consort, a long-legged goddess who has her left foot planted firmly on the ground and her right leg deftly slung around the god-man's waist. An advanced yoga pose for sure.

Between the consort's legs beneath her shapely buttocks I could see two small semicircles which on scrutiny revealed themselves to be the visible half of the male deity's testicles hanging there just behind her crotch. His godly organ, tucked neatly inside her, was not manifest. They were locked in sacred union, doing it standing up, there on the wall, subtly, expertly, elegantly.

IV.

The memory even now has all the flavour of a vivid dream, Corinne and I making love in the loft on the Main in Montreal under the sacred picture. It was less auspicious sex than the deities were having, perhaps, but for us in the human realm it was as perfect as it could be.

It was protected sex, of course. There had been a little discussion. Corinne didn't want to get pregnant and we both knew that on this occasion she could. I supplied the condom. I had been saving it for awhile. I hated condoms, but this one was a wise precaution.

We made love, revelling in each other's assertive gaze, lost in non-thought, unbound, unhinged, the usual. There was that elusive sense of recognition, the sense that I had known her before in some other realm. She was lost, babbling. *"Je vois jaune et rouge bordeaux...et y'a des étoiles pétillantes,"* stars effervescing on wine and yellow suffusing her mind.

Time passed in this way. "Don't come, not yet," she said at one point. I assured her I would not but asked her why she mentioned it. "I want that you keep loving me," she said, knowing from experience that men lose interest suddenly. In this situation she was fairly safe, though, because for me the latex sheath I wore prolonged the love, perhaps indefinitely.

But still I asked her if she felt like stopping for a while. *"Oui,"* she said and we took a break. We were still embracing, though. She was sighing and nattering, then laughing aloud at the absurd sounds she was making. She had a sense of humour.

She got on top of me and we fucked again. She arched back the way my wife never would because it reminded her of whores. I was sure Corinne knew all the love positions.

I imagine she was thinking of David because right in the

middle of her wild ride she says, "*C'est juste une relation amicale, Michel.* We are just friends, right?"

"Of course," I agree, but the truth is that at the time I believed we were doing something more decisive, endorsed by the deities on the wall. I feel myself falling.

I say, "The stupid condom makes no difference now."

"That's because I'm so turned on. I'm giving you my energy," she says. And so it seems. We mutter, we moan, we ululate, we are sexual throat singers, you know the scene. And then *au bon moment* she cries, "*Vas-y, Michel! Viens!* Please, I want for you to come!"

I am happy to oblige. I roll her over. The window is open, I notice. *Shaktipatananda.* There was no hurry but I knew where I was going and it was not to yoga class, not right away.

"Soon," I announce. "No, now, I'm going to come *now.*"

"*Moi aussi,*" she says, and simultaneously we are released.

We lie there in silence, temporarily awash in the warm, black, salty waves before a hard world dimly recalled surges up to shroud us. I thought of David, feeling the guilt. *I have stolen something.*

Because of the condom there was no danger of anything going wrong, we were both feeling quite secure on that score. But I was going soft and starting to worry about the thing slipping off so I asked her to stop moving. I reached down to grab the top ring of the rubber but could not locate it so I went further into her with my fingers while carefully extracting myself a little at a time. Still nothing. Finally I am out completely and the frigging thing is not there.

"Shit, it's still in you!"

"What is?"

"The dohickey, the thingy, the *rubber,*" I sputter. "Wait! I'll get it out."

In a panic she pulls up her knees, spreading herself wide. She is soaked, her hair matted. Leaning over her I catch the fragrance of incense, pine-scented, wafting in through the window perhaps, or residual in the apartment itself though I had never smelled it so strongly before. Hoping it is not the odour of some sacred conception I glance at the *thangka* and then my eyes flick to the futon under Corinne's thigh.

For an instant the crumpled latex is incongruous, as if someone else, Léa's partner perhaps, had left it behind months ago and I had just not noticed it. Then I recall the little break that Corinne had taken and the particular way I had rubbed my body against hers. It dawns on me that maybe I had not been perfectly hard the whole time.

I pick it up. It is empty, all right. Used, but not used, not employed at the right time. I show it to her. Her eyes widen, her face alters dramatically. "*Hostie!*" she says. "*Câ-lisse de ta-ber-nac!*"

I am saying, "Oh God, oh fuck, oh shit!"

"I *always* get pregnant!" she shouts and jumps up to run the length of the loft to the bathroom. I watch her bounce away and leap up to follow her, keenly aware that my diligent sperm were twisting themselves deeper into her by the second.

V.

There was some water in the bath where I had started to fill it earlier in the day, but it was cold. She had coopied down in the tub fumbling with the taps asking, "Which one is hot?" and I had turned it on full force. "It's too cold, don't sit down yet," I cautioned, but already she was in. Freeze, burn, whatever works.

Soon she was lying back in the hot bath, open to the healing flow, letting the water in, using her fingers. "This works, I know it does," she said confidently. I sat on the toilet watching, perversely admiring her despite the gravity of the situation.

She was calm. We were both calm. "I'll have an abortion," she said.

I watched her dry herself and then I got in the bath and she watched me and we got dressed and sat in the kitchen. I plugged in the kettle. I could see she wanted to leave. "I have a sick child at home," she said. She got up and pulled on her boots.

"Is this wrong what we have done?" she asked.

"There's absolutely nothing wrong *per se* with what we have done," I pronounced. "But the context..." I paused, not completing the thought. *The husband, the guilt.*

"I want to hug you," she said. She did, and she seemed perfectly fine.

"Sorry about the mistake. It was an accident."

"*Ça, c'est bien évident,*" she said. She believed me, that was good. I kissed her. Her lips were tight, she seemed worried. Then both of us froze.

The rapping at the apartment door was authoritative. Someone urgently needed to enter, it was that kind of knock. Whoever it was had already gained access downstairs. How long had they been listening at the door? Corinne moved on cat feet to the bathroom just off the kitchen area. The tub was still full of steaming water, the bathroom mirror was coated with condensation.

The knock came again, more insistent this time. The chain on the door was not fastened. I threw open the deadbolt while engaging the chain, using one sound to cover the other, and I opened the door the few inches it would go.

"David, hello! Come in!" I cried, loud enough for Corinne to hear, trying to sound happy to see him. I closed the door in his face, fumbled with the chain to gain precious seconds, then energetically flung it open. *Come in, my friend, I have just made love with your beautiful wife.*

"Is Corinne here?" he asked, politely stepping just inside,

glancing to his right. She was sitting nonchalantly at the kitchen table sipping cold coffee, a magazine open in front of her, her red jacket on. The bathroom door was closed but you could still smell the hot water.

"I was just going," she called out brightly, rising, moving toward us. She was flushed and excited. David was smiling a fixed, slightly caustic grin. His auburn hair was loose, falling over his shoulders. He seemed an artist's model for a contemporary Last Supper Christ. He spoke words to Corinne in a language I could not identify, let alone understand, though she seemed to.

"*Arrête-moi ça, là,*" she replied, laughing nervously. She went right to him, no goodbye kiss for me now. "Thanks for the coffee."

I locked the door behind them, quietly fastening the chain. I stood in a trance, listening to them talk on the stairs. What was that language? The bed was in disarray, the futon had a huge wet spot. The Dalai Lama grinned at me, first in an amused, supportive way but then derisively. Gestalting between interpretations I stumbled across the room and collapsed on the bed. I could smell Corinne. The deities on the wall were still hard at it, the yidam's wrathful mien untempered. In minutes I was asleep, cast mercifully into dreamless oblivion.

VI.

This is how I remember it. Corinne might have a different story.

The phone was ringing. There was a dim grey light in the room, a cold breeze through the open window. It was not late but so heavily overcast that the streetlights on St. Laurent were stuttering to life. From the voices and music in the background I knew she was calling from a restaurant or a bar.

"I'm very disappointed, I'm very hurt," she was saying.

"*Un instant,* I was asleep."

Monster Ovulation

"Why did you do this? You don't seem to care."

"It was an accident, I told you." The condom, I thought.

"I don't mean that," she said. "You took advantage of me." I was not fully awake and for some moments I thought she was making a joke.

"You seemed perfectly eager to me!" I said.

"I wasn't at all."

"Come on, Corinne, you were horny as hell," I reiterated, sure she would agree.

"You are in denial," she accused, her tone ominous.

"About what?"

"About the pain it causes, don't you know? Of course it doesn't cause *you* any pain, you think it's a beautiful, spontaneous thing. You think, 'I had a great fuck, *tant mieux, c'est tout.*' But the consequences are huge for me." She had raised her voice. "Do you understand? *Do you?*" There was a small pause.

"I'm not sure I'm getting your point," I said, cautiously.

"Don't be stupid, Michael. I mean that you are denying responsibility for your seduction," she said, pointedly enough.

"You don't see it as a mutual seduction?" I countered.

"Of course you would deny it. But you knew that I couldn't control myself, and you knew *when*. I told you I just wanted to kiss you and look at you, I didn't want anymore. You didn't want to hear that. *You preyed on me.*"

"You were *there*. You were into it. Are you denying *that*?" My voice was rising now, matching hers.

"I was feeling some things, yes, but I didn't think it would go as far as it did and you were just so ready to go *at* it, really quickly, right? I don't know why I have to explain this to you..."

"You went along with it, that's the point."

"Well, I didn't want to, I didn't want to at all!"

"Well I'm sorry but I was really enjoying myself and I could have sworn you were, too," I said. It seemed so obvious.

"*Oui,* I enjoyed myself at the time but I don't enjoy myself now, OK? It just wasn't worth it to me, OK? I went along with you *because I have no control!* You just don't understand my point, you don't get it at all, *do* you? I can't just leave your place and walk into this other life and be OK, although for some reason you think I can. You are not looking at reality. If you did you would take responsibility and not force things...." She paused.

"I see," I said, sensing that I was perhaps beginning to understand.

"And I'm probably pregnant, does that worry you in any way? You'll go to the Skala drinking with your friends, you'll have a really good time tonight. I'm not in that situation. I'm really fucked up in the head right now and I'm really upset! But that's all right with you, though, *isn't* it?"

She was in tears, now, hysterical. That word, I know. But where was the logic? I assured her that her being upset was not all right by me, but she seemed not to be listening.

Silence again. "Is your lack of control my responsibility?" I asked, softly.

"*Alors,* I won't bother to try to explain it to you anymore! There's no point, is there?" she fairly shouted, her voice bristling with exasperation.

No words, then, just the sound of her sobs while I struggled to make sense of this. I could not. Finally I asked, "What did David say?"

"Nothing," she said. "He said nothing."

"Nothing? Corinne, you were already arguing with him on the stairs. And what language was that?"

No response.

"What did you tell him?"

"Nothing. He knows nothing. I told him we were friends, that we had coffees together, that I liked you as a friend."

"Did he believe you?"

"I don't know."

"Well, how did he behave?"

"He wasn't happy."

"What do you mean he wasn't happy? How did he express his unhappiness?" No answer. "Tell me, Corinne."

"He...he...."

Long pause. I was thinking, *Oh Jesus,* over and over. She was crying uncontrollably now. "I want to see you," I said. "Where are you?"

"I can't see you anymore," she said, and hung up.

VII.

I did go to the Skala that night. The usual crowd had gathered. I pulled my friend Alan aside and told him the whole bitter story. Of course he only got my side of it. "She's flaky," he concluded after quizzing me for every detail. People joined us and we drank on, but I was hurting. Angry on the surface, sad underneath. That's me.

The next day I called her several times and again the day after that and maybe even the third day. I got her machine every time and I didn't want to risk leaving a message. She did not call me, there was nothing I could do.

I went back to yoga one more time. I was very uncomfortable even entering the building. I stood at the coat rack and took off my jacket and was about to unlace my sneakers when David appeared in the doorway that leads to the studio. I instinctively glanced over his shoulder to see if Corinne was there. She wasn't, or I couldn't see her, at least, but I didn't do a proper search as I quickly realized that David was fixing me with those eyes of his, with that sullen, magnetic stare he had. I stared back very nervous and afraid. After a second or two he shook his head.

That's all he did. He kept his eyes on me and shook his head meaning, No. *No, you can't come in here tonight, you can't come in here anymore*, that's what I took it to mean. It seemed very clear. It even seemed reasonable. I put on my jacket and left.

I was quite calm at first. It was done, it was done. But then I began to tremble. I walked fast up St. Laurent to Bernard, humiliated, my brain ringing with rage. It had begun to rain, it was cold. Over to Hutchison and south again, avoiding Outremont, avoiding the trees and the grass, wanting hard pavement under my pounding heels.

The ignominy of it. What right did he have? The little guru asshole. I wanted her, I wanted her out of his clutches, she was too much woman for that slick pseudo swami. Free her. Get her out in the bars, get some real religion in her.

I stopped at the Skala: old Greek men hove off drinking, foul smoke, no one I knew. I sat numbly with a *grosse cinquante* and slowly came back to myself.

For weeks I hoped she would contact me but she didn't. You can't force a person. I saw her a few times from my window, going in and out of the Centre, sometimes with him. I met her once more, about a month later, hurrying from a restaurant. Maybe she had seen me coming. We stood facing each other in complete awkwardness. She averted her eyes. "In case you're interested, I'm not pregnant," she said and with one small glance at my face, maybe to savour my reaction, she turned away.

I lasted in Montreal until the second week of December. My course had finished and although I had made some friends I had achieved no success. The weather had turned dirty, the decorations were up, carols were playing from cheap speakers on the Main.

I missed my boy. I wanted to be home.

D.J. Eastwood

In the Tent with the Macaroons

You sell. Weekdays, Saturdays, Sundays. Your clients, short, tall, stout, coiffed, beer-bellied, picky, wary, in pinstripes or blue jeans. You learned when to joke, swear, tease, lie, soothsay, grin. You choose the moment but always on their time. Twenty-three years at it; your wife hasn't asked about your work in what, say ten? Before that you think she cared.

She's at the sink, dish towel in her hands. In black mohair, tight, hips spreading, smart breasts, still the same curve you first caressed in the back seat of a green '52 Dodge. When she grabbed you, your foot slipped off the clutch pedal, jarred the transmission loose, you walked down Signal Hill, arm round her, one finger teasing the crease below the right nipple. You straightened at her front door when her father came at you, you can still smell the rum, see cut glass spitting light over a porch, hear words uttered about you that made you cringe. You think it funny he talks about it now as if you were brave, that he'd really only come out to pin a medal on your chest.

Your wife waves a gooey fork at you, says, you can't be serious.

You stare into a tray of baked macaroons. Think about telling her you always hated them, they are all air, the coconut sticks between your teeth and you have to eat about a dozen to feel like you've had anything. Why can't she make cookies with substance, like the ones you had as a child? You volunteer none of this, say only, a client arrived unexpectedly from Calgary.

This happened the last Saturday there was a game, she counters, and you promised the kids then you'd take them to the next one.

You shrug, offer, there will be other hockey games, besides, a sale will pay for their Christmas gifts.

She spits, they need you now!

You mumble, you'll make it up.

You make it up. That's what you do best. As a matter of fact, that's all you do now, everything you tell her is made up.

She has given you her back, you trace her bra line to the centre, wonder where the urge has gone. Your eldest ambles in, girlfriend in tow. She's in black. You admire his taste. He picks at a burnt edge on a white mound on the tray, teases his mother hoping she'll release one. You watch the younger woman, sparse with words, sparse with makeup. In your head you hear one word every time you see her enter a room. You won't allow yourself to say it. Your son doesn't ask for a cookie but for the car.

Your wife says, no, she needs to drive his brother and sister to the Leafs game.

Your son says, isn't dad taking them?

You hear your wife talk but watch your son look down at your feet. When he was younger he'd ask you anything, his bright face intent on the answer. Now you think he doesn't believe you have eyes left to meet. You explain while he bites a lower lip, his glance goes to the woman he loves. Hers goes right through him. He is red. You know they have talked. You tell yourself she is more what doesn't show than what does. You look at your son and know one day she will waltz away from him as if they had never met. You imagine your son's balls in her hands, her lips at his hard head, you imagine more passion in her than your son has ever known, you believe every bone in his body cannot stand against such strength, you think he wants a ring through his ear to match the one through her navel. He does not already have one because he fears the older woman in black, and, as far as she is concerned, there is no one in the room with her son right now. But, you tell yourself with a husband's prerogative, this is because she is in her forty-fifth year and is terrified of the power of that ring.

Your son turns, descends six stairs to the family room, the girl drops step by step behind him. Slinky, you think watching her, that's the only word for it, slinky. You go to the laundry room, slip your key into the cabinet lock, drink from Jim Beam until you feel the sting deep inside you. You lock it, explore your pocket, take out a mint.

You pause on the steps up to the family room. Your son's face, lit by a TV tennis match, blue. The girl, bored, lying on the couch, legs askew like she been tossed there. You imagine your face between her legs, the warmth, you taste mint, roll the white ball in your mouth, push it up against the roof of your mouth, move it about the way you would her clitoris. Your son senses you watching, lays one hand on her stomach, zaps a player into oblivion with a remote, says, let's get something to eat before Voodoo.

Voodoo, you say to yourself in the car. What the hell's voodoo, some weird teen ritual? Make yourself up like a zombie, inhabit the dead zone, stick pins into dolls and call up names you've learned to hate. Grow up, you say, pulling into Tim Horton's. You get three coffees. In the car you unlock the glove box, take out the silver flask. You roll down the window, baptize the parking lot with half a cup of Tim's decaf, fill it back up from the flask. Bourbon, coffee and mint, you croon, slipping into a French accent.

Your client works for a company that cements the pipe into the holes that the big oil companies drill in the ocean floor. You cannot imagine how they do it, decide to avoid the topic. You park on Victoria Street, meet him at number 66. You shake his hand while reading out loud the name on his nylon jacket, Schlumberger. You immediately imagine a slum kid stuffing his face with a burger.

He corrects you, that's Slumber J.

You see pajamas, see your son's girlfriend lying on the couch in flannels, the top all unbuttoned, pale skin showing, her eyes fixed on yours, you feel yourself growing hard. You shake, say carefully, Slumber J., then add in a southern drawl, sounds like a lazy ol' ranch somewhere out west.

We're run out of Texas, he says tersely, could we take a look at this place? I know we've got others.

You would have started in Wedgewood Park, new houses, Jacuzzis, two-car garages, broadloom, built in vacs. Oil clients usually like that stuff but the secretary said he'd left a message about something downtown, two-bedroom.

There's nothing worth owning downtown, you told her, besides, I don't have any listings down there, and, you added, anybody with the kind of money this guy probably makes deserves better. She suggested you show him 66 Victoria. You paused on your way out, remembered she just bought an old place a few streets over, on Cochrane. You smoothed it, told her he couldn't possibly appreciate the downtown's charm the way she did. The top of her breasts showed white under black when she bent and handed you the keys. Nice, you had thought to yourself, and made a mental note to buy her a drink or two at the Christmas party next month.

. . .

Your client examines the bathroom at the top of the stairs. You kneel by the vanity holding a loose wire. When he asks, you say you'll check with the renovator, then add, these old places harbour strange dangers. He sits down on the toilet cover, you look over at his groin, smell the dank musty aroma of a man who has sat on cramped airplanes for hours. You feel yourself stiffening, imagine him slipping down his pants, see his cock standing straight, taste swamp and salt in your mouth, feel the taut muscle of his body. The urgency of your hunger beads on your forehead.

The man stands, says, I want it.

You say, pardon?

I'll take the house.

On the way down the stairs you suggest he stop by and see the others, just to compare.

Son, he says, and you flinch, I know what I like.

At least ten years younger, running fingers tenderly over the old rail and newel post as you descend. You tell him you admire a man who knows what he likes. He tells you he loves quality. As you lock up you calculate how much this particular bit of quality will make for the woman whose name is on the Re-max sign. You only hear what he's saying after the second time. You tell him about the hotel dining room.

Seen it, he says dismissing the suggestion. He decides to wander, tells you to fax him the papers Monday.

The two coffee have chilled on the dash. You curse clients, half empty the cups on the street then fill one from the flask. You finish it, empty the flask into the other, stare at the digital timer pacing you. A half hour passes and suddenly you realize the hockey game will be less than half over, the kids will still have cookies left, you could buy them drinks, see the last period, one turn of the key and you could join them. Instead, you choose a walk, telling yourself that no one will know when you finished showing the houses.

You walk down Victoria, turn along Duckworth towards the center of town and its bars. You slip going down the stairs in McMurdo's Lane. A tall skinny kid in biker's leather stands outside the doorway of the Duke Of Duckworth watching you pick yourself up. Snowflakes garnish orange and green spikes flaying from the skin on his scalp. Your hip aches. As you enter the pub he asks for spare change. You wait until you are sure he won't quite hear, say, work for it, tiny cock, and chuckle to yourself.

Two bourbon later you navigate down the lane's slippery slope, cross over Water Street to the liquor store. A redhead at the counter wears gold-rimmed glasses and a soft smile that makes you want to hug her. You set the bourbon down and rub your hands together.

Some miserable out there, she says, kind of a day you'd like to curl up in front of a fire. Seventeen-ninety-eight please.

Yes, you think to yourself, a nice fire.

That will be seventeen-ninety-eight, sir.

You look up, realize you have been staring, make a show of taking out a twenty, pick up the bottle and leave.

Outside you are arrested by snowflakes falling like weightless popcorn, you stick your tongue out to catch them. A tinny carol pours up the street from Melendy's outdoor speakers.

Good old King Winch-the-slush, you sing, on the feast of Stephen. Onward, kingy old boy, you shout because you believe he's the only Christmas character jolly enough to get any sex on a Christmas eve.

Excuse me sir, says a woman's voice.

You wheel, blink. The cashier clutches her sweater close to

her chest with one hand and holds the other out to you. You imagine she could be the king's jolly wife.

You forgot your change, sir.

Her coins warm your palm as you calculate where you will go now. You decide Slumber J. has something in common with you after all. You both like to wander.

The powder in the air quickly turns to mush underfoot; your brogues thicken as you drift along Water Street. You step into a doorway to sip from your bottle. A group of six, shaven heads, army boots, miniskirts and open shirts push through slush, are upon you before you can move; they want to enter the store.

What-sa-matter old man, got no fucking manners, says a pimplefaced kid in army fatigues.

Younger than your oldest, he's immediately grabbed by a girl in black leather, Sorry daddy, she croons, Billy can be such a dick.

The boy purses his lips, makes sucking sounds.

You are about to express your annoyance but the whole group bursts out laughing.

You panic.

Don't laugh, you say, pushing through and retreating across the street to another, safer doorway, one blocked only by the condensation on its glass panel. You raise a middle finger to the kids, shout, fuck you. A bus cuts them off but you hear their jeers over it, so you swivel and push through door.

You stand on a wet patch of carpet surrounded by tables in the steamy air of a restaurant. A racing heart pushes bourbon through your mind like the wind does the fog. You close your eyes to gather your wits and a face appears, you think it is your wife's. It looks young, has the cashier's soft smile, you sigh, lean to accept its kiss.

A voice says, we're kind of full right now.

You open your eyes on a woman nothing like your vision, peach sweater, straps cutting into the flesh under it, hips hidden in a loose green skirt, a tray with two glasses of white wine balanced on her left hand.

Your feet, cold, heavy and wet, say they do not want to move but your voice does not inform her.

Would you like to wait, it'll be awhile.

Yes, you nod.

It'll be about fifteen minutes, maybe....

You interrupt, ask if you might have a glass of white wine while you wait. Enquire about a bathroom.

Yes, she answers, and, it's back there, in the corner behind the pillar.

It's a tiny room, barely enough room to turn. You pee looking down at your shoes, know that when they dry salt will rim the punched leather. You swear at St. John's weather, the roads, dig out the bourbon, sit against the vanity and drink. A knock pulls you from another dream. You balance against the walls as you go out, perch your hip against a glass cooler filled with desserts. The peach waitress spots you and brings over a wineglass on a tray.

You take it and ask, do you have a name?

Yes, she says, I do.

Before you can ask again she's gone. You rub your eyes, spot a blond head and an empty chair across the room by the pillar. You stumble over, ask if you might sit, do not wait for the answer. You close your eyes but this time the room inside spins so you open them, smile at the blond, ask, do you come here often? You drink through the answer.

Really, you say after you notice the silence, never been here myself, nice place. Listen, I mean, you look like a nice, then reconsider, did I tell you I sell, yep, real estate. Yep, real real estate. Listen...would you like some wine?

You wave at the counter, point to your glass, hold up two fingers. The blond eats a salad, you think the eyes are blue but they are watching a fork pick through the lettuce. You lean and grip the edge of the table.

Wow, you say, snapping your head to clear it. I was wondering...you begin but are interrupted. The waitress speaks to the blond, you hear, no, it's okay, I don't mind. Righteo, you say to yourself. You grin at the waitress who says, just let me know if he does, before she departs.

You lean onto the table, ask, you wouldn't know where a guy could get a little, you know. You brace for the response, quickly add, hash. Nope. Well, maybe a joint, coke, anything. The blond's voice leaves a gauze around the word no. Cagey, you think, so that's the game. You paw the table with a palm, tell her you've got a lovely family, nod, say four kids, nice wife, but you add quickly, checking to see if anyone might overhear you, if she were interested. Interested, you know, she and you?

You wait for an answer, shake the bourbon haze, stare. The eyes are blue, the shirt yellow with a button-down collar, a man's shirt. Jesus, you shake your head again, it's a bloody long-haired freak.

Goddamn kids you say to yourself, can't tell what they are anymore.

Hey, you say addressing the blond, if you don't want to, maybe you know somebody? A guy? A girl? With a floppy wave of your left hand you add, I don't even look anymore.

You sense something pathetic, the room, maybe the wine, perhaps the thin pasty face of the blond, a face that has no idea what life is really like. You have your own answers, why screw with another know-nothing kid, a waste of your time.

Pay, you say, digging into your pockets. Extract yourself from morality.

Pay! you say, you pull a ten from a jumble of bills, push it across the table, stand. You turn back, hover over the blond, keep the change.

You stand on the sidewalk trying to remember where you parked. The Calgary asshole, you say out loud, cheap bastard. You start singing as you sluice along Water Street:

>Oh I wouldn't live downtown,
>wouldn't live downtown for a million bucks,
>wouldn't live downtown cuz downtooowwwnnn
>sucks.

You repeat this until you get to the steps at the bottom of the courthouse. Two cabs idle beside a taxi stand, you choose one, drop into the warmth of the backseat. Cabby asks and you tell him downtown, he says you're already there, buddy. You say, drive. He tells you he can't drive without a destination. You know you know the street but it escapes your tongue, you tell him you parked the car by Calgary, he names Vancouver, Quebec, Charlottetown but doesn't know any Calgary St. You think of landmarks, oh, you say, the street that runs by the BIS. You settle into the warmth, wiggle your toes. Your eyes close.

Someone shakes you. You dig out cash, do not wait for change, step out into a parking lot and look up at the big building with its Irish flags and crumbling mortar. You know there is a reason you chose this place but you cannot quite pin it down. A second cab pulls in, its interior light goes on, you see a green-haired woman gathering dollars, the doors fling open, a short woman with a blue face steps out followed by a purple-headed boy. Two others get out, their hair reminds you of bad rainbows you once painted on the gym wall for a high school dance. You sniff. The blue woman walks lopsided, one shoe built-up, balances on the arm of the boy to combat the slush. They head up the steps. You holler, where you going? Imagine them all having sex. Sex with a bunch of geeks, you think to yourself, kinky. The green-haired woman says, we're doing Voodoo, wanna come.

Doing Voodoo you sing as you pee against the corner of the brick wall, doing Voodoo, what's that supposed to mean? Hollow-headed fucks, you scream against the cold and wet. Voodoo is it. Well, you say out loud, you're going to find them and climb into this tent with the macaroons just to see what it's all about.

You shuffle carefully over concrete risers that take you up Garrison Hill, hold the rail to control wet leather on black ice, stare at the couple who seem to walk miraculously up the paved path from the street.

Salt, you say aloud, but hang on to the rail anyway.

A line-up on the bleacher steps of the old Nickel Theatre confuses you.

Jesus, you tell a group of teenagers with shaven heads, this theatre shut down years ago.

One steps forward, thickly blackened eyes, white paste over her skin, you expect abuse but her voice floats out, it's used for concerts now.

You do not answer. She watches you blinking at the crowd. You ask almost apologetically, can anybody get in?

Sure, she says, but they better be up for it.

You climb one step and her words click. You turn back to ask but there's an empty spot where the group stood.

You climb the wooden risers that ring with childish hoots and taunts: fat boy thinks he's Zorro; where's your cape fat boy; let's see your rapier, if you got one. Then the mocking laughter. You shout inwardly that you live in Mount Pearl now, Mount Pearl! These steps and the downtown slummys have no hold anymore, none, the child you were then is dead, get it, dead!

A necking couple take your money. You want to ask her if it tickles more when he kisses her twat with that ring through his tongue. Instead you look at clear skin over her head and say, you'd be a blond.

She scowls and the guy says, crank off. You step through the old double doors and a ball of twisted sound smashes open your eyes, Jesus God you say, stepping round the passageway into a wire scream. You want to hold your head but you are stopped by bodies bouncing, spinning, twisting, slamming into each other. You see a small zombie woman fling herself like a panther against the flank of a big dark-haired girl in leather, they ricochet, swing together, the little one leaps, circles the other's midriff and locks her legs, they begin to whirl. The group parts as they pick up speed. Through soggy socks you begin to feel the pulse of the floor, it doesn't stop there but runs up your legs, you scream, not the scream you expected but something spectral, you are sure something wants to escape, you swing your arms wildly as if you are about to defend yourself from something you can't even see. You recoil from your own voice, step into the path of the small woman who has freed herself from the dervish. She thinks you are dancing, grips your arms, begins to pound her feet rhythmically into a floor that leaps to meet them, you scream again, she pulls your head down like a mother taking a child to breast and screams in your ear, fucking right on, man, right on! You come up like a child. Christ, you say, fading, sinking back under the balcony to absent back rows where neckers once copped their first feel. You pull the flask, drink. You steady, decide to leave but the music hacks into the smoke-filled blackness like rows of steel sawblades spitting bodies and body pieces into writhing heaps. You begin to rock, then to pant as if you have been running from something you cannot see, you turn to look, and, bang, the blades explode.

You think of your cat, then think you haven't thought of

In the Tent with the Macaroons 143

your cat in years. The geek from the parking lot shuffles through the crowd a few bodies ahead of you and you feel like you have run into an old friend, you stand and shout but it is only one more sound congealing in the screaming air. You wave at her, cannot believe her hand when it rises at her side and bobs back and forth like the toy dogs' heads that drivers put in their rear windows. You shout, do you want to dance, she turns palms up, then points to her ears and shakes her head. You shuffle through the crowd in her direction, a chant begins to accompany you, soft at first, voooodddddoooooovoooodddoooo, then picks up speed and power until a guitar cord severs it like a pig's throat. The geek bounces, tossing her body against gravity, against its own bent form and you think to yourself you have never seen anything so beautiful. She moves as if she has transcended grace, you shake your head, wonder how anyone so plain could suddenly transform. You halt in front of a treasure afraid to go forward or back, afraid you will rob the instant of its hold over you, a hold you don't understand but don't want to lose.

This time it is your youngest that you think of, maybe ten at the time but deciding to quit figure skating, your wife angry, the coach angry for she is obviously talented, you take her to MacDonald's because you do not know what else to do, expect her to cry, but instead, she says steadily over sucks on a milkshake, I did it right daddy, didn't I? You knew she did, you just didn't know how to tell anyone you knew. You walk to the geek, shout in slow motion what-is-your-name. She mirrors back, A-lice. Alice? you say! She nods. You stick your thumb up, wish you had a daughter named Alice because it feels like the most beautiful name you have ever heard. Then you realize that a name has entered you and you are ashamed because earlier you wanted to violate the body that bears it. You pronounce your wife's name and believe it is the first time in a long time that it has fallen from your tongue whole. Who is this woman, you ask yourself, turn back to dance but the song slams shut and the chant begins but this time you hear ZorroZorroZorroZORRO-ZORRO and a spasm shifts your body and you want to kick at the faces behind the words but decide to run.

The urinal is ancient, stained, like something on a Parisian backstreet, except that this one is both real and a part of a real memory. You know it, once stood looking up where you now stand looking down. Someone steps in beside you, a constellation of boy, needle hair, bald chest, studded belt. He zips, pulls his prick from its leather lips, lets it fall, throws his head back and sighs. You will not let yourself imagine him the same way you did your client in the bathroom on Victoria.

You sniff, take out the flask, tip it back into your lips. From the corner of your eye you watch the boy watching you. You think to yourself, one day he will be a priest, you are sure of it. You offer him the flask, he nods, zips, swigs, nods and leaves. You tuck, check that everything's in place, realize there is more belly than you believed. Fat, you say as you exit.

There are floating people on a jam of arms. They roll and tuck but never seem to drop. Heads pop up and down like the pistons on a churning human engine. You see one going high, high, higher until he is standing above all the heads, he is naked from the waist up, slender, fine-boned, handsome, he wavers, falls towards you, catches himself, is caught by the light. You see your son's face; eight hands hold his ankles. You want to wade into the swarming mass, stand ready to catch him but he lurches sideways, disappears, then pops back up on a bed of outstretched arms. You see a woman bobbing behind him, she leaps, leaps again, grabs and kisses him, then is flung onto the mattress of hands with him, they chase one another along its unsteady plane.

You are not prepared for the flood this opens within you. As mad as it seems, you believe this place has life, a form of life that you abandoned somewhere a long time ago. You sink to the floor not caring about the bodies bouncing around you. The man with the naked chest pushes past, you grab him, say son, a stranger looks down at your hand on his wrist, then at the woman who still follows him. She shakes her head. He flicks your tie, says, dude. They dissolve into the sea of legs around you.

You scream again because you know no one will hear it and it won't matter; a specter is loosed from your throat. You wonder if it is the bourbon but are too frightened to believe one way or the other, then you hear a voice saying, what you could not protect for years is never totally lost. You realize that it is your own voice. You do not know what it means but you think you will remember it tomorrow and understand, things will be different, you feel sure.

A metallic vortex spirals from the guitars, the drummer dumps them over the edge, a cheer, hoots, then again, slowly building, a chant. Alice and the bathroom guy with the constellation of spikes appear and pull you to your feet, the hall begins to throb.

You scream at Alice, who are these guys?

She cups her mouth and shouts in your ear, then spells the name on her palm.

Deja vu du, you mouth back to her.

Right on, nods her partner, then chants voodoo, voodoo, voodoo.

You stare hard at Alice. Try the word once. A smile drops from her lips. You smile, listen as your voice rises and joins the strange, reckless chant.

Jim Quilty

Learning to Breathe

No. First you must learn to breathe.

What's the matter with the way I breathe now?

Rain flecked the silence through the window blinds. His eyes settled on the enormous cock of the Japanese guy kneeling beside him. Old Lai brought up some phlegm before he spoke.

"When you were younger, you were probably taught to inflate your chest when you breathe. Yes? 'Keep your back straight when you walk.' 'Throw back your shoulders like a soldier on parade.' Did they tell you this?"

The whole shaft wasn't visible but, veins, tendons and all, it was thicker than the guy's forearm. Payne nodded his head, Uh, yeah.

"This is wrong. It's hard work keeping your balance if you have to walk around with a chest full of air. No balance, no walking. So when you breathe, don't fill your chest. Fill your stomach."

He smiled. Anatomy was obviously not a strong point in oriental education. He ran his eyes along the folds of the geisha's robes. Layers of orange, yellow, and white disheveled beneath her lover's onslaught. The caption said The Geisha's Seduction—chosen to decorate the month of April—had a springtime motif. Not because of the impending copulation, but because the woman was wearing 'springtime colours.' Payne shook his head. Such careful attention to details of colour, but no sense of the human body.

"But you have to fill your chest when you breathe. That's where your lungs are—"

"No, that's wrong too. Listen. Put both feet flat on the floor and close your eyes."

Gusts of wind were whipping maple branches, wet on the far side of the blinds. Payne shut his eyes and did as he was told. Lai began walking him through the breathing exercise he had taught him the last time, the old man's voice becoming irrelevant as Payne focused on what his body was supposed to be doing.

So far it seemed that t'ai chi had more to do with imagination than exercise. You had to forget all that stuff you learned about internal organs and see yourself as a hollow vessel full of water. Inhaling wasn't about inflating a pair of fleshy balloons, but pushing a large ball down from the top of the ribs to the base of the abdomen. You had to inhale through your nose and concentrate on pushing this ball down as you did so. When the ball was flush against the inside of the abdomen, the tip of your tongue was supposed to rise naturally to touch the roof of your mouth.

You exhaled through your mouth by letting your tongue drop from the palate and allowing the ball to rise back to the top of the ribcage. You were somehow supposed to remain relaxed throughout this contortion.

"In through nose. Out through mouth," Lai's voice emerged from his concentration. "Ball sinks. Ball rises. In. Out. If you okay don't talk. Just nod your head."

Payne nodded his head into the long pause. The worst thing about it was the old man's voice. It always sent him back to the Chinese shopkeepers and restaurant owners who lived on the outskirts of his childhood. Incongruous small-town adornments, so different from the Chinese in Vancouver for some reason.

Payne sat and breathed. Guts and mouthfuls of half-digested peanut butter toast reformed as a bathtub full of children's toys.

Chinky chinky chinaman sittin on a fence
tryna make a dollar outta fifteen cents

Plastic shovels and building blocks dissolved into streams of muddy water running in waves down Victoria Street.

what comes out've a chinaman's arse?
rice! rice! rice!

Pooling in the gutters of Commercial Drive. Bits of silt, stirred up by the wind and rain, pushed lazily aside by the passage of the ball up and down.

Light was starting to shiver impatiently between his eyelashes. "Okay. I think I've got this thing down, now. Should I stand up?"

Lai sighed again, as though bored with this question. "No. This only half the lesson. Second half next week."

"It's supposed to rain again tomorrow—"

"Next week. Use this week to practice. But when you do, don't try to remember everything I've told you. Just concentrate on breathing. Now you can ask your question."

His upper lip twitched into a sneer. Breathing from your stomach. Practising what you've forgotten. He felt like he was in a 1970s kung fu movie. He shoved the ball down.

"Look, I can probably cope with learning to breathe today. Don't you think? I mean, I was supposed to be learning to walk, wasn't I?"

"Mistah Payne. I already agree to give lessons...your way. It your money. But the student doesn't say how he will learn."

"So I can learn to walk next week?"

"No breathing, no walking. You understand?"

He sighed to himself and nodded, "Okay. Talk to you next week, then."

He waited for the dial tone to drop into his ear before setting his phone back into the cradle. He pushed the ball down again, thinking vaguely that he should have tried videos.

It is an early work, this place. The dusts and pigments of it pressed deep into your pores. The years have applied many coats since then. Spaces brighter and more comfortable colour you. But your organs, your fingertips know this place. It is a hill, and from this distance it could be the flank of an enormous dog. But you do not yet have this distance.

She is walking diagonally over the rise. A woolen cardigan that isn't wool. Dark blue, with odd buttons. Buttonholes scissored wider, then darned so the bigger ones will fit through. Funny black shoes too small for her feet. Fur round the ankles. Walking.

Early spring, high above the nearest houses. The grass long and straw-brown, snow-pressed flat and damp against the loam. But there is no snow. Walking diagonally up the hill, on the left sides of your feet. Walking west, towards a cottonwad sky, towards water.

"Kin ye show me d'indian livin'room, mam?"

"Yes my son. Come on, now."

Walking towards the rocks.

She stops now and again for you to catch up, to prise up an old tire or board. Picks the odd berry to entice you. You're too easily lost in the flattened grass. The grass too long to be pulled erect, too tangled. Always so much more underneath to pull on, until it's cold and slimy on your fingers. You make sure she doesn't notice as you wipe the discomfort off on your pantleg. Near the hem, worn clean of colour from walking, beyond notice. You've just learned that your pants are not only orange and brown and blue, but plaid too.

"Come on my son."

"Kin ye show me d'indian livin'room, mam?"

The door slammed him back to now. The sound of her boot heels reopened his eyes to the calendar. The samurai and the geisha still teetering on the brink of coitus. Payne wondered if the expression adorning the geisha's face—still intent upon the samurai's grossly swollen member—was meant to be bashfulness, or dread. He stopped breathing, filled his chest with air, and smiled as she turned the corner.

"Hello MacMillian."

She smiled back, surprised, and dropped wet coat and umbrella in the middle of the floor. "Oh you *are* home. I buzzed but there was no answer. So I just let myself in. That okay?"

"Of course it's okay," he lied. "That's why I gave the keys to you. Must be broken."

"What?"

"The buzzer." He dropped the phone back on the coffee table and pulled her onto his lap. "How's Ma and Pa MacMillian?"

Her face soured. "Awful. Still threatening to murder Felice. Mom asked after you, though. 'Where's Jeremy these days?' she says. 'Have you two broken up?'"

"Still fond of me too, I see." He eyed the puddle advancing toward them from her discarded rain coat. "Why do you suppose she can never remember my name? No Geoffreys in Coquitlam, or what?"

"There's not a lot of things in Coquitlam. I think she does it deliberately, though. Doesn't like the way we talk to each other in surnames. She says it makes us sound like lawyers."

He carved a name plaque out of the air with his left hand. "MacMillian and Payne Barristers and Solicitors. She's right, you know."

Carmen was scratching a patch of eczema on her wrist. Precisely where his hand had rested a moment earlier. He sighed, "You told me to remind you not to dig at that. You told me to tell you that it just makes it worse."

She brushed the flakes of skin off her lap and unwrapped a nicorette gum. "Fuck off. Mom."

He didn't risk saying the thing she'd told him to say next. Best to avoid unpleasantness. As he watched her teeth clench carefully into the gum, he slid a hand inside her tee-shirt and up the dry valley of her back. Outside, the rain had oscillated back to a patter without rhythm. "Have you showered today, then?"

"'Fraid so." She stopped her hand before the nails could reach her wrist again. "But I probably missed a few spots. Do you feel like it?"

When he returned from the bathroom with the family-sized bottle of Lubriderm, Carmen was already standing naked in the middle of the living room. Fists clenching nails into her palms. "These blinds are filthy. Don't you ever clean them?"

Payne smiled grimly. "Not in my nature. My family's Catholic."

He pumped a palmful before setting the cream down, and began to rub it into her back with both hands, stomach muscles tightening as he worked the residue into her shoulders and arms. "Is this any worse since you moved back home?"

Carmen nodded, eyes closed.

"You think it's the cat? Or your parents?"

"Hard to say. Felice drives my allergies crazy, but that's got nothing to do with the eczema, apparently. Mom just drives me crazy."

Another few squirts were pushed up each leg from ankles to knees to thighs before being massaged into Carmen's buttocks. "This is my favourite part," he grinned. "Reminds me of Mam kneading the dough when she was making bread."

"You really know how to charm a girl. You don't hear me comparing your cock to silly putty, do you?"

Sliding his fingertips into her cleft, he let a greasy thumb slip up her anus to the second knuckle. "Ooops."

"Funny thing," she murmured, head tilted to one side. "I don't think I've ever had eczema up my ass. But you always—"

"An ounce of prevention."

The bottle was slippery in his hands as he filled both palms with moisturizer for the third time. He blew her nipples hard before working his thumbs in small circles from her breasts to her hips, then up and down each rib, and back to her shoulders. Breath shallow, Carmen had tugged his trousers down to his ankles. His shirt was hanging from one wrist.

As he stepped out of the puddle of clothes she'd made, he wiped a lick of Lubriderm from the piece of metal piercing her navel and arced it round her forest of pubic hair. He noticed, then, that he'd fallen back into Lai's breathing exercise. "Feel better?"

The rain was drumming in waves off the pavement outside. She took his cock in her hand and manoeuvred him back to the chesterfield. "I'll tell you later."

The next week it was sunny, and Payne found himself at the base of another forty-foot ladder, the west wall of a West End condo. Not looking up. It was built on a hill, this condominium, and it had taken four two-by-fours to level the ladder. He climbed up two, three rungs and jumped a couple of times. With each impact the guide wheels leapt away from the wall nervously. He sighed. The first tall ladder of the season always made him wish he'd taken university more seriously.

He hoisted the oversized bucket and began the ascent. The closer he got to the twenty-foot mark the more elastic the aluminum became, the more shallow his breathing, until waves of vertigo were tearing at him, and he was left clutching the ladder tight to himself.

He kept his eyes closed until the ladder calmed itself. Then, focusing on the stucco he was being paid to conceal, he climbed until the bumps and ridges began to inch closer.

A few weeks into the job he'd discovered the best way to cope with the heights was to pretend he was climbing down a ramp to the ground. He didn't even know he had vertigo until he arrived in Vancouver, after he'd taken up painting. It took him longer to realize just how much the walls were like patches of earth.

His first job of the season had been restoration work. A clapboard bungalow in Strathcona. When he'd arrived at the job site with his ladders and high-pressure hoses to do the pressure washing, he found the old layers of paint had bubbled in the spring heat, as though the family had been seething inside for decades. Barely contained. When the water struck, layers of old paint flew off like lengths of asphalt liberated in a tornado. But no matter how much came off as he'd advanced, there were always peninsulas, islands that resisted the water—primitive Africas, Japans, the odd, attenuated Newfoundland even. Water remade the walls into topographies. Maps.

Payne had taken to painting right away. It satisfied his compulsion to hide old imperfections. Like when he was a teenager, using a blue crayon to colour in the scuff line left over when his mother took the hem out of a pair of jeans. But lately pressure washing had become his favourite part of the work.

There weren't many jobs that paid you to alter geography. By the time he finished, it was never any place he recognized.

He suspected he wasn't a typical painter, and he never let on why he always volunteered for prep jobs—miserable wet business in a climate like Vancouver's. The older guys he occasionally worked with didn't refer to the walls as anything at all, though if they split the clapboard or gouged it with a scraper, they always called it the same thing, fucking whore.

At the start of the season a university grad had worked a couple of jobs with him. She had liked to refer to the house as 'text,' and she'd go on for hours about how the water marks and streaks of birdshit were actually discrete bundles of meaning. The penknife engravings of adolescent lust, the waxy red smears of youngsters experimenting with lipstick, the black pockmarks of attempted arsons upon the clapboard, were all, she said, unexpected subtexts. But she hadn't lasted long.

The rock has shed its grass and loam now, abrupt and steep. She takes your hand and leads you up over the first boulder and down the other side. Touching it leaves sand on your palms and you smack your hands together like she does to remove it, even though you like the feel of it. And tufts of green stuff are hiding in the pockmarks and ridges the wind has cut in the surface of it. The wind blowing a single lonely tone in both your ears as she pauses, bandanna billowing, her forehead furrowing into lines you want to touch.

"Any mora dim berries, mam?"

"What, my son?"

You smack your lips. "Any mora dim berries d'eat?"

"Later on, my duck." And she smiles different lines at you and leads you over the wide field of stone ridges. Ridges that you now think must have looked like her forehead when she was thinking. When a drawstring would pull her eyebrows together, clutch her mouth tight, until she looked like a spring coiled before violence. Darning Pop's socks when he didn't come home on payday, or hemming the pants your aunt Minnie had sent because Harvey had grown out of them and there was no point in wasting them, was there?

Then she makes a noise in her throat and you both turn into the wind. She feels your shiver before you do and bends over to pull the zipper up to your chin. You put your fingers on her forehead, and she smiles it smooth for you.

You follow her along the wrinkles until they fall into the shallow depression she was looking for.

"Are you tired, my son?" she asks you suddenly.

"Nope!"

She jumps into a hollow that would look like a stone boat swamped in an ocean of rock. Taking you around the middle, now, she lowers you down to the flat bottom. Then runs her fingers along the steps and benches that wind and water have carved, eventually finding the one to sit on. "Dis was my favourite chair," she knots her arms in front of her to repress a shiver.

When your palm touches the rock you can feel the wrinkles it has pulled tight to flatten itself for you. You fold the lines of your hand over the dust it's gathered.

"Is dis d'indian livinroom?"

"Yes, my son, dis is her."

"Dis is d'indian livinroom, mam?"

"Yes, my son, dat's what I said."

You sit down next to her. "Where's da TV?"

Payne was breathing deeply from the stomach now. An Indian living room made of granite. He re-dipped the roller into the viscous white stuff until it was sopping and rolled it against the screen to wring the excess. Face inches from the stucco, he could see all the spots that the prep guy had missed—at forty feet the pressure washer had barely splashed the aging paint. It was still hanging, moist as broken blisters. He fingered his scraper for a second and he could feel Carmen's eyes, quizzical as his fingers plied her desert skin. Abandoning the thought, he retrieved the roller and started to slap it on quick. Up here there was no one else to know.

About an hour after Payne got home, Carmen, working with a bar of Pears and a pot scourer, had scraped the paint from both his arms and his chest. She was now applying herself to his knees and shins rising out of the water like corrupted islands.

"Am I hurting you?"

"No sweat," he smiled through closed eyes.

Times like this it occurred to him how much Carmen would appreciate the fine art of pressure washing, if not painting per se. Unfortunately for the profession, she was studying how to rob graves for a living. Payne never called her a grave robber to her face, of course. The one time he had, at a dinner party packed with archeologists, she'd stabbed him in the back of the hand with a dessert fork. Carmen was handy with sharp metal instruments generally, not just trowels and pickaxes.

"Have you been here all day, MacMillian?"

"Didn't get back till the afternoon." She squeezed some water over his leg. "It's easier for me to study here than at home."

"Anyone call?"

"No one called when I was here." She looked up from his knee. "But there was a really weird message on your machine."

His eyes opened. "You checked my messages?"

"I thought mom or dad might've called. Because I didn't get home last night. Is there a problem—"

"What was so weird about it?" He felt his jaw clench.

Carmen didn't know about his eccentric relationship with Lai, of course. She would not be sympathetic.

She sat back on her haunches, brows furrowing. "It was just weird. Some old Chinese guy. Sounded like he was trying to hypnotize the answering machine or something."

"Crank call?" he suggested hopefully.

She submerged the pot scourer and tried to shake out the stray bits of paint beneath the surface. She spoke without looking up. "He asked for you by name."

Carmen was better at not asking questions than anyone he knew—her discreet digging instincts, he assumed. He wanted to sink down and hide beneath the paint shavings. Instead he pulled his knee into the bath water and sat up straight. The water swirled around him like the domed winter scene that used to squat on top of his parents' television every Christmas.

"I'm taking some lessons."

She pulled the scourer out of the water and wrung it out before starting to extract the bigger paint scales with her fingernails. "Oh?"

"Yeah. T'ai chi. You know, like slow-motion karate."

Her upper lip quivered slightly. "Don't be so condescending, Payne. You know very well Tom taught t'ai chi at the university. Why's the guy leaving messages on your answering machine?"

"That's how I'm taking the lessons. Over the phone."

"You're trying to learn a martial art over the telephone? That's the stupidest thing I've ever heard."

"It's not a martial art. It's more like meditation."

"Of course it's a martial art. Tom used to show me the applications for the movements all the time." She paused, a distant smile playing on her lips. "He used to say t'ai chi was the most effective way of dealing with someone up close."

Payne tugged his testicles closer to himself. He was feeling a bit too exposed for another anecdote about Tomaso Bandaras—the ex-boyfriend that Carmen had beatified the day he dumped her. Halcyon Tom—who had tee-shirts from every worthwhile experience life had to offer—tended to lurk around the corridors of any conversation that centred on Payne's competence.

"Yeah? Well that's Tom. I'm not interested in dealing with anyone up close."

"No kidding. Why are you studying it, then?"

"I told you. Meditation."

"Meditation." She grimaced. "You're not going new age on me, are you Payne? I thought when Newfies felt meditative they just got drunk."

Payne was staring at the ceiling. He heard Carmen wheeze as she inhaled. "Besides, how are you supposed to learn something like t'ai chi without face-to-face instruction? How can some guy claim to be able to teach you how to move when he can't even see you? The guy's obviously a fraud. Phone him and demand your money back."

Damage control, he nodded to himself. He wouldn't tell her that he'd insisted on taking the lessons this way. He pulled himself out of the water.

"Where are you going? I haven't got all the paint off you yet."

"I'm feeling a bit waterlogged," he grunted, reaching for a towel. "And I'm just going to get covered in it again tomorrow anyway."

He put up no resistance when Carmen declared she was going home for supper. As the door shut behind her he turned on his heel to check the phone message.

"Mistah Payne. This Mistah Lai calling. You should be sit in comfortable chair and close eyes. Remembering ball pushing down from ribcage to stomach as breathing in." He paused. "Now imagining ball rising snug to ribcage as breathing out. Breathing in through nose, then touching tip of tongue to roof of mouth." He paused. "Breathing out through mouth allow tongue relax. If you okay just nod. No questions till I say."

He glanced at the answering machine and paused the tape. "Yeah, I always ask for clarification from tape recordings."

Payne sat in the chair and practiced breathing the way Lai had told him to forget. For some reason his accent seemed worse today. After a couple of minutes he touched the machine with a fingertip to continue.

"Good. Only thing wrong is you are slouch in chair. Americans always sit opposite of walking. Imagine spine is stack of plates with string running through middle. If too big curve in spine, plates will falling. Reach up to top plate in your mind. Take string between thumb and forefinger. Pull it so plates are in perfect stacking without touching. Okay?"

Payne straightened his back and immediately felt uncomfortable.

"Remember, though, only part of stack having tension is string. Plates themselves all relax." He paused. "Now. Let ball rise. Just before easing ball back into stomach, imagine a bead of light floating two finger width below navel. When you ease ball back into stomach, bead of light push down, over private parts, round bottom and up back, through neck. Not stopping till it meet tip of tongue touching the roof of mouth. If you can see, just—"

There was a loud meep from the machine. It could only tolerate so much t'ai chi instruction. He sat rigid, trying to work out the last set of instructions. The machine meeped twice more.

"As I am saying. Bead of light displaced down, over private parts. Around bottom and up back, through neck. Not stopping until it meet tip of tongue touching the roof of mouth." Lai paused. "Imagine bubble in a carpenter's level. It move down and up as balance shift the water."

He used to play this game. The red wooden level was a fetish for his father, struggling for years to build a family house that looked like other houses. Driven horizontal into the hillside, airtight against the gales. A house that couldn't breathe. Payne used to look for the bubble in that level. Shaking it. Trying to break it in two. Lai cleared his throat.

"If you can see, just nod."

He nodded, eyelids fluttering under the strain of remembering.

"Good. Now. Let ball float into ribcage. When tongue drop from the roof of mouth, imagine bead of light drift back to that place below navel. Don't forget to breathe. You okay?"

He inhaled. "I'm okay," he exhaled.

"Good. This is how we breathe. You practice this week. Forget instructioning. Breathing only. Save questions next week."

She shimmers before you now, sunlight blown through clouds. The wind driving icicles into your ears, drawing hot water from your eyes. Dissolving her. The ground starts to shift under you, curling you into a ball, but the rock juts hard into your stomach.

He felt a bead of water running down the bridge of his nose, then the thrashing of feet against his thighs, nails sinking panicked into his chest. He grunted and tried to pull the sheets closer.

"*Fuck*," she wheezed. "I'm suffocating. Would-you-get-off-me!"

Fists drummed his chest. His lips tasted salty. He tugged one set of eyelids open as Carmen tore the sheets from their moorings and threw them off herself.

"Payne!" She punched him again. "Wake up!" The bed shook from the force of her scratching.

"Whatsamatter."

"You're a goddamn furnace. You've got me fucking drenched. Again."

He rolled away from her and felt the damp sheet constrict around his chest. The bed vibrated furiously. He prised open his other eye and switched on the lamp. Her stomach, arms, and breasts were already clawed a violent red. "Stop scratching yourself so hard. You'll rake yourself raw."

"Fuck yourself," she sobbed. "What do you expect me to do?"

Payne tossed the blankets off and pulled himself into a sitting position beside her. He didn't argue. What else were you supposed to do when your boyfriend's sweat makes you itch like a bastard. And it was happening more often lately. These nocturnal migrations of his across the mattress. Trying to pull her closer, usually crushing her against the wall in the process. He bent forward and blew a stream of cool air against her thighs, hoping to dry the sweat before she could tear at herself anymore. She pushed his face away.

"Stop that. Bring me the Lubriderm, will you? And my cortico-steroids?"

He pulled himself up and staggered to the bathroom. It was inevitable in a way, he supposed. He'd learned about Carmen's pet allergy and the eczema during the opening round of seduction. It was only later he found out how deep her problem went. If the doctors had it their way, she'd be getting by on a diet of apples, potatoes, and turnips. She was allergic to every other food item, though she assured him only nuts and seafood would hospitalize her.

By the time he'd come along to displace Jason, the hangnail-chewing anthropologist-boy, she'd already told the doctors to go fuck themselves—she was going to live her life the way she wanted. At the time it had just made her more desirable to him. Since then Carmen had started reacting to his sperm, and the spermicide in his favourite condoms. Hard to be surprised, then, when she developed an allergy to his sweat too. Was it possible, he wondered, to become allergic to someone's skin, his breath?

When he returned from the bathroom, Carmen was sitting in the living room, dragging on a smoke, eyes intent on the calendar of oriental pornography. The pinks and reds of April an ironic reflection of the chaos of her flesh. Deep scratches scored her from shoulders to shins, making it look as though he'd had a go at her with a cat-o'-nine-tails. The eczema would feed off these wounds.

"You want a nicorette?"

"Fuck the gum," she exhaled, raising the cigarette. "I've got everything I need right here."

He nodded, mute. Nicotine gum wasn't such a good idea anyway. On top of everything else, the cartilage in Carmen's jaw was disintegrating, something called ando-mandibular joint disorder. Gum-chewing just accelerated the problem. Never mind her nicotine allergy. He sat on the arm of the chair next to her.

"Look, MacMillian. I'm sorry."

Her nails scraped insistently against the silence. There was blood on the cigarette when she brought it back to her mouth, but she took the creams from him gently.

"It's not your fault." She unscrewed the jar of steroid and dabbed it lightly on the deepest scratches. "It'll be better once I get back into the field."

Payne's stomach twinged. His shoulders tensed. "I didn't realize you'd decided already."

"There was never any doubt, was there? I can't afford to

pass up the work even if I wanted to. Besides the only time I feel human is when I'm away from this city."

He pumped a palmful of Lubriderm and held it out for her. "If you want to go back into the field that's your decision. I'm just afraid you're romanticizing this Supernatural-BC thing a bit. I mean, how much better could living in the bush be when most of the natural world throws you into convulsions? What if it's not as good as you remember it?"

Carmen laughed, her smile lingering over some private memory. In the semi-darkness the black-clad samurai was a storm front stalled over the elegantly rumpled layers of his partner—the two of them no closer to consummation than they had been at the beginning of the month. When she spoke again it was them she was talking to.

"You know the worst thing about working in the field? Deciding where to dig. See, when you're working in pairs you can only cut this narrow shaft, so your chances of finding any interesting remains aren't really that good. Mostly all you find are bone points."

Carmen's eyes hadn't wandered from the samurai's cock. Is she making a joke? he wondered.

"You find so few artifacts, sometimes you can't help but feel you've left something behind. Even after you reach bedrock. You're fifteen or twenty feet down and the most interesting thing you've uncovered is a singed tree root, but you know that there's something. Just a few feet to the right. Still buried. Makes you want to go back and start over."

Payne was pushing a fingernail through the residue of Lubriderm in his palm. The thinner it was spread, the more it collected in the lines there, highlighting them. His head nodded slowly, silence buzzing expectant in his ears. He inhaled,

"There's a memory I have that's like that. It must've happened ages ago. It started coming back to me a few weeks ago.

In pieces. Something happened. Maybe nothing happened. I can't see it still. Know what I mean?"

Carmen didn't respond, though her smile had faded. He shouldn't be surprised, he thought. It wasn't like he ever confided in her about anything.

"Carmen?"

"Sorry?" She turned to face him. "Did you say something Payne?"

He started smearing the rest of the moisturizer into his leg. "I asked where you'll be going this summer. To work, I mean."

"Back to the Island. Same site as last time."

A set of passing headlights squeezed through the blinds and searched the floor for them. After a minute she smiled again and touched his arm. "Nothing to worry about, you know. Tom's not even out there anymore. I hear he's back in Vancouver these days."

Still covered in yesterday's paint, Payne stood in the middle of his living room, breathing. Arms bowed out from his shoulders, fingertips nearly touching, reaching around an imaginary tree trunk. His legs were spread wide, his knees bent, pelvis thrust out lewdly, as though to embrace the tree with his cock as well.

No, not tree, he reminded himself, a post. A Jaysis big post. This latest contortion, Lai had insisted, is how we stand while we breathe. "We," he had been told, must master this stance, the standing post it was called, before "we" think about walking. And, of course, walking was only preliminary to learning the 108 movements of the t'ai chi form.

He took his mind away from the internal ball, circling bead of light, stack of plates, and imaginary post long enough to check his knees. Lai had intimated that allowing his bent knees to extend out past his toes would cause grievous, but unspecified, damage. He pushed the ball back down, held it against the inside of his stomach, and another basso fart blurted out of him. Must be the hummus he'd had with supper yesterday.

He'd had to work last week, so Lai had left the latest set of instructions on the answering machine again. He'd thus avoided Payne's questions about his indecisive accent—he was much easier to understand that day. Within a few minutes he was sitting down, legs shaking violently, his entire body slick with sweat. This standing-thing was worse than climbing a forty-footer.

April had finished, but he still found himself gazing at the Japanese couple. He leaned forward in the chair, enthralled by the disparity between the size of her feet and his gonads. His feet were invisible. Were orientals more naturally inclined to balance, he wondered, to tote around these prodigious sexual organs on such tiny feet? And what was it about this scene of near-sex, the potential coupling of black with orange, yellow, and white, that especially characterized April, anyway?

Carmen had been sleeping at her parents' place lately. When she went home the last time, Felice was nowhere to be found, and dour Mr. MacMillian had refused to discuss the cat's sudden disappearance. Carmen had dropped round one evening to vent her disgust to him, but then she'd gone back—home was apparently the preferred option now that she could breathe the odd gulp of air and get a night's sleep without having to scratch. The rain had slackened to a gentle drizzle. Lai should be calling soon.

The living room is far below you now, and there is nowhere else to climb. She pulls a bright yellow square from her bag and shakes it until the wind gives it arms, making it into a coat. Tugs your arms through the sleeves and fastens the smell of new rubber around you. The drawstring has pulled her face tight as she bends close, telling you to keep this on, to dare not move, no matter what happens.

"Do you hear me Geoffrey? Stand right here."

She lowers her eyes and leaves you alone. Wind lapping tears cold against your cheeks. You twist your palms into your eyes to squeeze the water away. Stiffening yourself as she has stiffened against the gale, you cross your arms tightly around your stomach as she has knotted hers. Pushing your toes into the stone as she wavers to where the rock stops and the sky begins.

The phone rang. Payne's palms were sweating as he picked up the receiver.

"Mistah Payne. Good today you at home again. How do you finding the standing post?"

Broken English rattling through mucous. Payne sighed inwardly. "Exhausting. Sweaty. Listen I—"

"Is good you are sweaty."

"Oh? Why's that now?"

"Sweaty mean you have chi flowing through you strong, but confuse—" Lai paused to hork up some phlegm, then smacked his lips. "Some time it mean your body clean out toxin. Also good."

"Yeah? Cool. I've got a question for you, though—"

"My assistant said you were have problem with standing post."

"Assistant. What assistant?"

An inscrutable oriental pause buzzed over the line. "I am instructioning you some days only. Some time you talking to my assistant, yes?"

"But you...he always introduces himself as Mr. Lai."

Static was slowly emptying out of the silence. It sounded like Lai had taken his mobile phone out to the balcony. "This is wrong. I will make talk with Mr. Bandaras about this."

His stomach curled into a fist. Another t'ai chi instructor named Bandaras? "Look," he said quickly, walking toward the window until the phone cord stopped him. "I don't want...your assistant."

"But you already have learn from him. Yes, Mr. Bandaras should have tell you his name, but he know–"

"If I agree to see you face-to-face for these lessons can I deal with you personally?"

He heard something like voices in the background. When Lai returned to the line, Payne couldn't tell whether he sounded confused or pleased. "This can be arrange. But first, you tell me how standing post is feeling."

"Like I said, sweaty. Wrapping my arms around that imaginary post-thing doesn't keep me from losing my balance, either."

"That not post purpose." Lai made a grumbling sound in his throat. "When you stand, you push against the ground with your feet. Yes?"

"Of course. That's how you stand up, isn't it."

"No. This wrong. Striking balance too hard if fighting the ground. Balance needing roots run deeply."

"Then how are you supposed to keep your balance if you're not standing on the ground. Like if you're up a ladder–"

"Same thing. Balance needing deep root. No root, not balance."

"Or walking. Over rocks, or something." Payne could hear children screaming energetically in the distance.

"People balance like tree balance. But tree root run outside. So. For balance, tree grow down as far as it grow up."

Fuck! He shook his head. Why did the old bastard always have to fall back into this oriental murk?

Lai turned away from the children and his voice disintegrated into the sound of electronic tins tumbling down a flight of steps. Then he heard Lai inhale, "Strength lie in root. So. In t'ai chi we say, when in doubt, sink."

. . .

You have never been so far above the ground. From this distance she is no more than the clothes blown rigid around her. She is standing still at the edge of the rock, body straining forward against the air. Held back by unseen hands, the clouds around her torn, bleeding a cold blue.

You open your mouth to bring her back, but the breath is whipped back into you. From here, feet pushing against this rock, fingernails dug deep into sweaty palms, you feel alone for the first time. So you forget your promises and start moving toward her.

Your feet throw themselves against the ground until the shock of it is shooting up the back of your head. The air wails in your ears, clawing dry against your throat as you run. It rushes up inside the yellow coat, pulling against you. But you pitch forward until half her face is visible again, thrust forward into the wind.

And you do not know this woman balanced on the edge of the cliff. Eyes set upon the distance, face patient, waiting for the gusts to release her. Her face as wet and smooth as your own. As though the wind had washed her free of ridges too.

Pain wrenches your ankle from beneath you now, and the rock throws you headlong into the wind. Here, free of the ground, your mother smeared into a blur of grey and blue, the wind pauses long enough to inhale. So the rock takes you back, kicking the breath out of you, so hard all you can do is close your eyes and wrap yourself around it.

Payne was still sitting on the floor, forehead against his knees, when he finally heard the phone ringing. His hands left moist impressions of themselves as they came away from the hardwood. Palms felt as though they had just sprinkled flour on the table, ready to work the dough. He picked up the phone without slapping them clean.

"Payne? It's me. Tried to ring earlier, but your phone was busy for ages."

The dust made the cheap plastic slippery in his hands. He could hear Carmen kissing smoke from a cigarette filter.

"Since when do the MacMillians allow the apple of their eye to smoke in their living room?"

"I'm not calling from home," she exhaled. "I'm at Tom's place."

He gritted his teeth into a smile, "Tom's place! Perfect! How is Mr. Lai today?"

"Sorry?"

"Just ask him. Tell him Mistah Payne want to know how Mistah Lai is today."

The sound of conversation mumbled in the background for a couple of seconds. "Tom says he doesn't know what you're talking about either. What are you talking about Payne?"

"Bandaras...Never mind. It doesn't matter now." He walked the phone to the window and examined his blinds. Carmen was right. They were pretty scummy.

"What doesn't matter?"

"Did you ever notice how you call me 'Payne,' but you call Bandaras 'Tom'? Why do you suppose that is, MacMillian?"

"Did you get a knock on the head, or something? Why do you call me MacMillian? That's what we do."

"That's just it. I may call you 'MacMillian,' but I've been thinking of you as 'Carmen' for months now."

"You're being pretty obscure, Payne. You okay?"

"Yeah yeah, I'm fine. No. I'm not fine. Look, I need to talk to you. What are you doing today?"

"That's why I'm calling. I'm going to be running around for

the rest of the day getting ready. Tom's driving out to the Island this weekend, so I'm getting a ride with him."

He had been grinding his thumb and forefinger into one of the muddy metal slats. His hand fell away now, leaving a moist thumbprint.

"This weekend. Carmen, today's Friday. Tomorrow's the fucking weekend."

"Jesus Payne, what are you getting upset about?"

"What do you think I'm getting upset about? I've seen you once, maybe twice in the last two weeks. I haven't slept with you in almost a month. Every time I think about touching you, you flay yourself alive, and I feel like shit about it. Now you're telling me that you're leaving town tomorrow for five Jaysis months with Tomaso fucking Bandaras."

He heard a click at the other end. She hung up on me, he thought. Eleven o'clock in the morning at Bandaras' place. She must've already slept with the fucker. He wiped a palm on his pantleg. The bastard probably doesn't even sweat.

"Carmen if you hung up on me—"

"You'll do what?" She palmed the receiver and raised her voice into the other room before returning. "I thought I'd save Tom the embarrassment of being in the same room while you insulted him."

"He's got bionic ears too, does he? Where are you now? The phone booth on the corner?"

"In the bedroom."

"Of course. Where else would you be?"

"Payne where the hell is this coming from? You've known about me going back into the field for months now–"

"Wrong. You've known about it for months. For me it was only a distant possibility until a couple of weeks ago. It's not like you actually tell me about what's going on in your life or anything."

"You're nuts, darlin'. My life's old TV compared to what I know about you." She exhaled impatient smoke into his ear. "You know what it's been like sleeping with you for the past month? It's not bad enough being marinated and steamed every second night. There's got to be some kind of frustrated mother lust going on too."

"What—"

"—hands all over me while you're callin' for you're mam. I'm not used to that shit from my lovers, okay? Call me weird but that's just the way it is. Been waiting for you to tell me what the hell's going on with you, man. To mention it in the light of day, even. But you're talkative as a fucking stone. As usual."

"Carmen, no. You've—"

"You've got issues you want to work out on your own. That's fine. So happens I've got a few of my own right now. I hate feeling like an invalid, okay? And it just makes it worse that you're always being Doctor Mom for me. Even playing doctor stops being sexy after awhile."

"Yeah? Is that where Bandaras comes into it?"

"Geoffrey leave it alone will you? Tom and I're friends. Besides. If I went back with Tom I'd feel more of a cripple than I ever could around you."

Payne stopped short, unsure whether to feel reassured or insulted. He pulled down on the cord and the blinds opened with a clank. In the far distance he could see traces of snow on the mountains, still defying the rains.

"Carmen there are some things...I want to tell you about them. But not on the phone." His eyes fell back on his thumbnail, the drop of paint there dried in mid-trickle. "I've got some paint on me needs getting rid of."

"Carmen, eh?" She sounded intrigued. "So you *do* remember my first name. Do you have any pot scourers left?"

The rubber coat tightens under your armpits, and you are yanked back. The rocks swirl dizzy and impatient beneath you until your feet are again pressing gently against the ground. Her eyes are more round, now, more brown than anything you've ever seen.

"Joe Jaysis. I tought I told you d'stay where you were to." Her bandanna has come off, loose curls blown flat in the wind. A deep crease slides between her eyebrows. You reach up and push your finger into it.

"You went'n ripped a hole in d'knee of your new trousers, now." Water is tumbling out of the corners of her eyes. She turns you around and squeezes you back into her.

There is nothing but her chest heaving behind you, and blue sky before you. Far below, blue becomes black and the clouds turn to stone.

She pulls you closer, and you sink between her shivering thighs. You watch the water make brief lace around the edges of the faraway islands. Sitting here, her hands clutched warm and dry around your own, you wonder what it is you cannot see.

Claire Wilkshire

Visit

They've made a banner for the airport—WELCOME HOME NICOLE on a huge sheet of newsprint—Eric has drawn balloons which are squiggles of different colours. They watch the arrivals door and Sarah feels silly holding the banner, which was her idea, but because of the banana she ignores that feeling. First the Friday afternoon businessmen, back from a week in Toronto, heading straight for the taxi line, home to a clean shirt and supper. Last weekend Sarah came home ravenous in the early afternoon and ate a banana which tasted so sweet and substantial she wanted another, but two bananas seemed silly so she had something else instead, bread and cheese, an apple, and she woke that night full of longing, tasting the sweet solidity between her teeth. What she longed for was not the banana now, but to have eaten it earlier. Sarah concluded that silly things should be done regardless, that silly is a poor reason for not doing something, and so here she is holding one end of the banner and helping Eric hold the other and scanning the now thicker stream of people, one coming toward them and smiling, Eric pulling on Sarah's sleeve and saying "Look Mummy, is that Nicole and Meg?" and Sarah explains again that Meg can't come this time but he's right, it is Nicole, looking different, the clothes not ones Sarah recognizes, the briefcase alarming—this is an academic come to give a paper, not an old friend visiting—but it's fine about the banner after all because she is plainly delighted, it was worth it, and here she is now, dropping the briefcase to hug them and the more Sarah looks the more it is Nicole after all, yes, the same, and she is glad of that.

"I have something in my pocket," Nicole says by the luggage carousel. She's short; Sarah always forgets how short until they stand side by side and Sarah sees the top of her head; to put an arm around her shoulders, Sarah would have to tilt down sideways, but as the minutes pass it becomes clear that this is nothing unusual—the tilt can be managed comfortably, Nicole was this short before, this is how it has always been, except that Sarah has forgotten (what else has she forgotten?), and now she sees Nicole in her mind's eye in a long black coat like a cape with a stand-up collar, a red beret, she wore that coat for years, shopping downtown on a December afternoon with the snow deciding to drop all of a sudden, wet flakes smacking their eyelashes, brushing down their cheeks, and Sarah remembers seeing from above the small tab poking out from the snow on top of the beret.

Eric is staring at Nicole's pocket.

"It might be something for Eric. If he looked in my pocket he might just find something there for him."

The boy reaches tentatively for Nicole's blazer, pokes his hand in, comes back with a hand puppet.

"Oh look, a moose!" He sidles over to the other pocket just in case, pulls up the flap, peers down. "I quite like Kinder eggs."

Sarah thinks about asking if Nicole still has the coat, a full cut, the fabric like felt only softer, but it was years ago, the black coat must be long gone now; she always thinks Nicole's clothes are new because she hasn't seen them before.

"I love you," says Eric. Nicole, startled, smiles hugely and squats down to eye level.

"Oh sweetie, I love you too."
"No I was just talking to my moose."

Nicole glances out at the morning and makes some sort of remark; everyone laughs, and she pulls the curtains smartly shut. She's showing overheads in a classroom, talking about molecular structure to a roomful of people, mostly men, all scientists except Sarah. The overheads appear to show an assortment of gumballs joined by toothpicks. Sarah would like to know whether a molecule is really a thing—is it matter?—or a metaphor for a thing. Obviously the images on the screen are representations of molecules. But are the molecules themselves figures for something else, and if so, do we know what? Because, Sarah thinks, if we don't know exactly what thing a molecule represents, if that thing could be mere hypothesis or speculation, then the gumballs and toothpicks might just be images provoking us to imagine something that isn't, mnemonics prodding us to remember what never happened.

Nicole is not talking about this, though; she's explaining about chiral and non-chiral somethings. Without actually understanding, Sarah hears the the precision of language, the clarity with which she sets out her data: Nicole can wield a semi-colon with the best of them. Sarah will have to ask about the molecules later. By the time they have lunch at a table outside Auntie Crae's, though, she's forgotten the question.

"You'll never guess who I saw." Nicole, tearing open a crusty roll and cramming it with dilled Havarti. She takes a bite. "Wanda Crummey."

"No."

"She's at Dal on contract."

"Wanda. My Lord. It's been a long time." Sarah sees the three of them—herself, Nicole and Wanda, wobbly with drink—standing in a tight huddle in Wanda's parents' kitchen, the parents in Florida, frozen strawberries in a blender. They are talking about their fathers; Wanda is crying, her tears falling onto the front of Sarah's shirt, the strawberries whipping around and disappearing into slush. Daquiris. Something Wanda had not said to her father, or the father had not said, Sarah's hazy on this, but it was about loss, the unsaid thing a continual source of regret because although it could still be said, the moment has passed and it's no good any more. Wanda's tears, the droplets flattening into small dark spots scattered down Sarah's collarbone. Over the years Sarah has felt that particular regret rise sporadically, like a cough, as she's thought of Wanda and her father and the moment irretrievable, and wondered whether Wanda still thinks of it, Wanda whom she has not seen for more than a decade.

"She started this new thing with her personal life a few years back," Nicole says. "She decided it was important to trust people. To give and give and not worry what's coming back to you. She said you might get screwed the odd time but so what, it's worth it, and most people are more trustworthy than you think."

"Geez. What did you say?"

"You know Wanda. She just proclaimed this at the coffee break. I didn't know what to say." Nicole looks at her watch, sweeps the crumbs into a paper cup, pulls on her jacket. "Any chance of a run later?"

Thumping along in thin June sun where the boardwalk tucks between the lake and the base of a dumpling hill, weaving though the Saturday amblers, the speedwalkers, wheelchairs, strollers, they're talking about a couple who have just separated.

"Women don't leave men," Nicole announces, "unless they have another guy lined up."

"Or another woman," says Sarah. Uphill. Nicole, panting,

manages a sleazy wink, sweat dripping into it. "It's not true, though," Sarah adds. They argue a little. "She wasn't seeing Richard until after."

Nicole raises an eyebrow.

"Well. OK then, Elaine. Elaine had no one lined up." Elaine's reception, a buffet at the Battery: Wanda Crummey was there, and Nicole. Elaine had beckoned Sarah and Paul over to the head table: "You guys eat whatever you can, you hear me? It's a set rate. Go back for more." Elaine, who has always been practical, even prim, leaning across the table, palms pressed flat on white linen, tossing the veil out of her face, whispering gluttony. Elaine knew what she wanted, worked for it, made it happen. Then she left her husband, or they split up, in any case she moved to the mainland and he did not: the impenetrability of couples.

"Elaine doesn't count," says Nicole. "What time shall I leave the wine and cheese? I want to be there for Eric's bath."

They've stopped at the yield sign across from the cemetery, checked their watches, leaned against a bench to stretch. At one time they were always going somewhere, leaving one place for another. These last years, movement seems more often circular. Running around a lake. When Eric was six months old, Sarah took him to Toronto for Thanksgiving weekend: she and Meg walked him round the block at bedtime to get him to sleep—the stubbornness in him, no nap all day and they walked for nearly two hours, around and around, Meg creeping ahead every now and then to peer into the stroller and announce that his eyes were still open. Sarah's not sure of the implications, whether they no longer have destinations, or the destination is the place where you are. She stands on one foot, pulls the other up behind her bum, grabbing Nicole's shoulder to steady herself.

"What about the banquet?" Sarah says.

"Shag the banquet."

"Excellent. Come home at eight then."

Twenty minutes later, in the shower, it occurs to Sarah: maybe women should leave men more. Maybe there are hordes of women moored to the wrong men. Bound by inertia to guys they could take or leave. Maybe as many as there are women dying for the right guy to come along—possibly the very guy whose wife, considering him, thinks, Ho-hum. It would be useful if these men could wear some identifying mark.

Nicole kicks off her shoes in the porch and plants a brown paper bag on the kitchen table. Upstairs they run the bath and strip Eric off in his bedroom. He peels out to the hall and down to the bathroom, a streak of white, a tiny bum, hops up on the step and tests the water with his toes. When he's clean and splashing around with his boat, they bring the wine up and sit on the floor in the hall, backs propped against the doorframe.

"How are things going with Paul?" Nicole wants to know.

"OK. He takes Eric Fridays and Saturdays, usually. He pays child support. We only talk about Eric. It's. What's the word?"

"Amicable."

"Amicable. That's what it is. We just don't have anything to say to each other anymore."

Eric asleep with the puppet clenched in the bend of his elbow, a set of antlers rising and falling with his breath. They tiptoe away. Sarah sinks into the arm of the couch, a bowl of tortilla chips balanced on her knees, and snorts: "My type? I don't have a type."

"You do so. I could pick out your type a mile off."

"What's my type?"

Nicole takes a handful of chips and wanders over to the bookshelf, pulls out a photo album, crunching in a considering way. "Older," she announces. "You like them older and smart."

"Get out."

"No, it's true." Nicole and Meg can tell Sarah things about herself that have never occurred to her but that she knows immediately to be accurate. It's like puzzling over a photograph of someone, being told, That's you all over—and finally you recognize yourself.

Sarah rubs the stem of a wine glass between her fingers. Pulling out of the driveway that morning, she'd hooked the corner of the bumper on a wooden post. She's looking at the photographs with Nicole and thinking about their run, about Nicole approaching the boathouse, in the home stretch, bending her arms at the elbows, raising her palms as if waving to the crowds which might have gathered on each side of the path to cheer her on, spreading her fingers to let the air pass between them. This is something Sarah remembers, this gesture performed quite unconsciously when Nicole is tired, an expansive gesture, one which suggests not only confidence of being accepted in the world but also the desire to communicate, to engage. Sarah's thinking about Nicole raising her hands like this, about the way the bumper hangs now from the front of the car, whether it might fall off, that Paul, who shares the car, will be furious, that she needs to buy diapers.

"Look," says Nicole. Underexposed snaps of a sleepover at her house—her parents' house—just outside town. January 8, 1983. Six girls. They're eighteen or nineteen, university students. New dark blue jeans with stark white socks, long cotton nightdresses. Sarah wears a big T-shirt, bare legs partly covered by a sleeping bag, Wanda's and Elaine's arms around her shoulders. "Oh," Nicole sighs. "I loved that T-shirt." In another shot Nicole sprawls dramatically on the couch, head flung back and almost out of the frame, her calves huge in the foreground. Sarah can't remember exactly what they did at these sleepovers. Listened to music. Ate cookies and chips. The excitement, the intimacy of it, six young women eating and talking and brushing their teeth together, sleeping in a pile in front of the fireplace. Telling all. Fifteen years ago there was nothing they didn't know about each other.

Nicole takes a long look at the living room of the house in which she grew up and reaches for another album.

"Oh," she says, "I talked to Mom and Dad. You're invited out for supper tomorrow, you and Eric. I'll spend the night and they can take me to the airport in the morning. You don't have to come; I said I'd let them know."

But, after all that, what do they know of one another now? Of Wanda almost nothing; of Elaine even less. Sarah has no idea what kinds of things Nicole and Meg think about from day to day, what they eat for supper. What do they fight about, and how are they with one another when they're fighting? What do they understand of Paul, of how her life has changed—how she has changed—do they notice a difference?

"We'd love to come." There was a time when "we" meant Sarah and Paul. Now it's Sarah and Eric. And Sarah and Eric will make the drive out of town, past the airport and the lake; they will keep each other company and Sarah will tell him of other such drives, often in winter after dark, the way the house appears suddenly, dipped down from the road, the warm amber of candlelight trickling out over a bluey white yard from windows stretched along the front of the house, how often they have made her welcome.

"So how are your folks?" Nicole inquires.

"Great. They had their kitchen redone."

"Didn't they just do that? The oak cabinets?"

"According to Mum that was twelve years ago."

"No way."

And Sarah is pierced by a stab of affection for Nicole, an affection which feels almost like grief, for the way she can recall in an instant Sarah's parents' kitchen: how often does it happen that a friend can do this, can say: I remember that day, in high school, eating sandwiches on the grass outside the portable buildings, so it must have been May or June, and your mother came to pick you up in a green dress?

"We're getting old," says Nicole. "Pass the chips. That classroom where I gave my lecture: know what that made me think of?"

"What?"

"Greek and Roman mythology. Second year. Dr. Armstrong talking about his hat blowing off at the Acropolis, about mistranslations. Eve's apple and the Golden Fleece."

"What was the mistranslation?"

"Don't you remember? It wasn't an apple at all, just fruit. Everything we think of about apples and sin, all resting on that word 'apple,' only it was the wrong word. And the Fleece might have been a fruit too, he said, and you and Wanda were late that day, tracking snow into the classroom with your huge orange boots." Sarah smiles. They have sunk back into opposite ends of the couch, into a drowsy companionability, full of food and wine and ready for sleep but not quite ready to get up.

"Nic."

"Yes."

"You don't still have that black coat, do you?"

"Which coat?"

"Never mind." Those boots, Wanda called them her moon boots. They'd been housesitting at a geodesic dome out of town—that's why they were late, looking after the greenhouse, their first task in the morning the care of seedlings. Stumbling out of the house in nightgowns and rubber boots, warm, humid greenhouse air, turning on the lights over the seedlings, stroking the fluorescent strips as they'd been instructed until light spread along the tubes—sluggishly, as if it too would have preferred another hour of sleep—cool glass dusty under their fingers, weak bursts of white, the cylinders warming gradually until the entire room filled with light.

Mark Ferguson

A Drowning

I watched him drown. The boat was far too close to the shore. There was engine trouble. I could see him working furiously trying to get it started. The seas were huge and the punt drifted in. All at once one swell broke, all round him, she went over, and I saw him leaping and thrown clear. Next I saw him there shocked in the water, but swimming evenly, fighting it, swimming away from the rocks, staying on top of the water, the white foam all over his darkly clad form like an otter in a brook. The next swell picked him up and swept in onto the low cliffs, onto the big black splintered rocks at their feet. Down he went a first time. I thought, I won't see him no more, but I was wrong. He came up a few yards shy of shore. I was shouting then. He was swimming mad out of there, swimming for his life, and another swell rolling in. It broke early, running down onto him like an avalanche for eighty or a hundred feet, a white wall tumbling and rushing forward to drown him. I saw him watching it come, paddling calmly out toward it and then I saw him duck under just as it struck where he had been. Smart, I was thinking, smart, but he was gone under a second time. I waited. The sea rose and boiled then sank away and back. The punt was already smashed, caught high up in the teeth of the land with tons and tons of water pouring back into the sea, off of the rocks and cliffs. The splintered wood of planks and torn brown strands of kelp in the blue-green.

He burst from below a second time, like a shot, his arm first, punching into air, swimming before he was even back on top of the water, swimming out to sea.

A third swell came then, larger than the others, I saw him see it. I saw him stop thrashing forward. I saw him turn sideways in the water, and look to the land, sizing up his chance. On it came. My arms jerked up—like a spasm and involuntary, waving for no reason really, a human impulse, a need to be recognized, to identify to him that I was there, even in the extraordinary circumstances. At all costs, waving only for him to notice me, to know that I was a witness. I did not speak, was not shouting, only my one big wave of both arms up over the head once. I left them up there, nothing but the helpless arms. I saw him then seeing me. He stared at me for one moment, held me in his eye, and there was no reproach, and no terror then, but something. Resignation maybe, like a tiredness, him knowing for an instant that I was something, a part of something back on land that he was really an incredibly long way off from. Never would he know it again. He was into something altogether different now. The connection between him and me, between his living breathing self and me, was pulled so thin and so taut in that moment, almost non-existent, not much longer now. No noise from him in the rueful moment, or maybe it was buried in the crashing seas and the jeering wind. And no noise from me, or maybe was I calling? And the speed was funny, the thing happening so slowly.

He went back to what he had been doing, what was really occupying him fully by then. He'd watch the third sea and then he'd watch the land, the sea, the land, and the sea seemed almost insane to me. Incredibly enough it seemed to keep on mounting, to keep growing, getting huge, getting heavy and dark—I know waves always do that when they come to the land—but this one time, this wave seemed ridiculous and wrong; it was breaking rules, the laws of waves or the rules had changed for that moment, and the fact that waves should rise up and break themselves onto the land seemed just then completely wrong, nothing only ugly and stupid. He looked so calm floating in the water, beautiful. As the beginning of the swell reached him, rising, I saw him treading calmly, now facing the land, his eyes fixed steadily on it. He must have chosen a spot he thought that he might just make, where he might just climb out of the wave and step magically back onto the land, soaked but safe. His whole thinking right then was determined by the concentration on that one wild hope. Then up he rose, and up he rose with the terrible sea. It rushed, it positively rushed on in then, gaining speed as it fell, and he had the whole crest to himself, that's how he rode in.

The world becomes utterly mute then, no sound, nothing, and I am the deafest one of them all, so utterly deaf it brings tears to my seeing eyes. That is how totally silent I remember it being. I see his face, his mouth open in a shout, half shock or surprise, half terror, his arms out meeting the crazy canted walls of rock, disappearing. I wonder can he still see his spot, can he still see that place he will land himself, step out of the sea? For how long does he think it will happen, for how long does he hold out, hold on to that one thought? Is it to the very last?

He was gone under for the third time, he disappeared completely then. He was out of sight and I never saw him then and he didn't come back up. How quiet was it? That total silence still when I turned away after a long time and he still hadn't resurfaced. I glanced back a few times, slowly climbing and clinging to the scrape and still no sign and a few times when I looked I thought, There. But when I looked a while it would just be a piece of wood or a this or a that. It stayed quiet like that for ages all the way back, and even when I got back, their voices at first were barely audible. They were talking but their voices were all really flat-sounding and seemed a long way off.

First person I met was John Mortimer waving from down a small pasture, feeding a horse out of a brin bag. He shouts and I barely make him out. "Beautiful," he says, "Beautiful day." "Yes," I say. Because it was—it was still sunny and very breezy and dry and not too hot and it felt like it'd keep on like that another day or two for sure. All the women had their laundry and their fish out. I went home, told Dad and I stayed in the kitchen there with Mom and she got me some bread and jam and some tea and he went on to tell everyone else, to go and get a boat, try and find his body. The little cat had got in again, walking around the kitchen, meowing for supper. We ignored her for a long time till Mom said something offhand to her, and we had a little laugh, not paying attention then, and then Mrs. Abbott came in looking really very sad.

Lisa Moore

Afterimage

We are on a yacht in St. Pierre. Maureen's boyfriend Antoine has invited us to go sailing but there's something wrong with the engine, so we remain tied to the dock. The marina is a blast of white sails and the blue is very blue. We lie on the deck and suntan. I have a book by Marguerite Duras open on my stomach. Maureen and I read most of this book one night three years ago. A short novel about a seventy-six-year-old woman of great literary fame who attracts a thirty-six-year-old lover.

We read it in the kitchen on Gower Street during a snowstorm, taking turns reading aloud while the headlights of fishtailing cars swept the ceiling and the velvet funk of pea soup rose from the stove. We were overjoyed for Marguerite Duras. Way to go Marguerite, we yelled.

But now, three years later, the story seems very different than I remember. The young lover is bisexual. Has affairs with bartenders in a nearby hotel. He seems to be terrorizing the novelist, who is too old and proud and drunk to do anything about it. She spends all her money on him and waits for him to bring food, sometimes going hungry. How had we mistaken this for hope?

I'm also hungry. We spent a lot of money at a local shop, but most of the food has been eaten. There is a florid pink sausage pebbled with lard, and a can of duck. We're too lazy to go back into town. A package of biscuits from Norway that hasn't been opened. For a long time nobody talks. Then my husband lifts his head from a faded canvas pillow, and looks one way, then the other. He puts his head back down, rolls his shoulders.

He says, I've just had a very strong memory of a bus ride in Cuba.

I say, With the wheeling eagle in the ravine.

He says, Not that bus ride.

I say Maureen's name. She doesn't move. Then, very slowly she sits up. She says, Isn't sleep strange, it overtakes us all, whole cities—the activities just stop for hours. It's just struck me.

Think of all the dead people, I say.

Antoine's hand emerges from a hatch, waving a baguette. Then his head appears very near Maureen's thigh. He bites her and she squeals. He beats her stomach with the baguette.

We eat the Norwegian biscuits and dip the hardened bread in cardamon tea in enamel cups without saying much. The fresh air has made us all sleepy. The white sails float on the insides of my eyelids, orange with a violet outline. For a while, there's commotion while a giant yacht ties up next to Antoine's.

The three sailors are dressed in Helly Hansen fleece, royal blue, red, yellow. A woman of perhaps forty with a long mane of steely ringlets raises the American flag. The flag flutters weakly and then wraps itself around the mast, like a barber pole. A white styrofoam plate lifts itself off their deck and floats in the water. They each pause and look at it. Then they step over the deck of Antoine's yacht to get to the wharf.

As he steps from Antoine's deck, one of the Americans loses his shoe. Maureen tries to fish it out with a long pole, but the shoe begins to fill with water. Antoine climbs over the side. He inches his back down the creosote timber of the wharf with his feet jammed against the yacht. It looks like he will either be crushed or fall into the filthy harbour. A speed boat passes and the yacht moves closer and the space for Antoine is very narrow. The American woman in white pants clutches the arm of the elderly man. The man removes a white baseball cap and rubs his forehead with the back of his hand. Maureen smokes and her hand trembles near her mouth.

All this for a shoe, says the man.

But Antoine scrabbles up, spider-like, and holds the shoe in the air like a trophy. He does a little bow and tips the shoe letting the water spill out.

Early in the morning I go to the yacht club to shower. I meet a woman and child from France, the family who tied their catamaran onto the American's yacht during the night. The woman gets out of the shower and isn't in a hurry to cover up. She has a tattoo of an orange and black butterfly in the concave dip near her hipbone. She scrubs her daughter with a thick white towel. The room is full of steam, and the fruity smell of shampoo. The child has the same blonde hair as her mother, shiny and pale like mashed banana. She tells me she has been on the catamaran for five years. They have been all over the world. Both the children were born while they traveled.

When will you stop? I ask.

We will continue for a long time, she says.

Maureen wears her sunglasses. We have finished the Norwegian biscuits. In the big black lenses of Maureen's sunglasses the ropes and booms and masts all criss-cross like a cat's cradle. She is crying and the tears slip under the plastic frames. I can't get a straight answer out of her. She has her arms wrapped around her knees. I sit up on one elbow and wave the book at her.

I say, This is nothing like what we thought.

She turns and the sun, which is setting, catches in one lens of her sunglasses and it burns a dark piercing amber and she ducks her head and puts her hand over her eyes.

She says, I wanted you to see this life.

It's foggy the day we leave. My husband shoots a video of Antoine on the dock as the ferry pulls away. He is wearing a navy and white striped T-shirt like a real Frenchman. He waves, and does not stop waving until he is engulfed by the fog.

Maureen and I met him in a bar last summer. He was wearing a faded fluorescent pink undershirt. He has an orange beard, tufts of orange under his arms, and a long orange braid. He told us that on her death bed his granny made him promise never to cut his hair.

Why would she do such a thing?

So I would understand the weight of a promise.

We watch him climb the rigging. His bare feet curling over the skeleton of the sails, a great height over the deck. His wiry body a part of the spare geometry.

Antoine's brother visits Newfoundland from Nigeria where he's been studying giraffes and getting his pilot's license.

He raps the brass knocker on the front door and steps inside. Sunlight flashes under his arms and between his legs and the door closes and the hall is dark. He stands, not moving. I am in the kitchen with my hands in the sink. I walk down the hall to greet him. He's wearing a straw hat with tiny brass bells on the rim and patterns woven in wine and dark green straw. His face is so like Antoine's that for a moment I think it is him, playing a joke. I hold out my hand, he grips it, soap suds squish through my fingers.

Any brother of Antoine's is a brother of mine, I say. He tilts his head quizzically, and the bells jingle through the empty house.

He sleeps in the living room on the couch. There's a french door with no curtain and he sleeps in his briefs with the blankets kicked away. He finally gets up and I don't know what to do with him. With Antoine, misunderstandings could keep us talking for hours, but this guy has a firm grip on English and I'm at a loss.

Okay, stay still, I say, I'm going to paint you.

His knife pauses over the bread. A gob of marmalade hangs along the serrated edge. I do portraits in ink on wet paper. The thing about ink, as soon as you touch the brush to paper you have decided the course of the drawing. First, I am looking into his eyes. I am thinking about the shape of the eyeball, and the size, how far the eye sinks into the face. How the shadow slopes over the bone of the brow—if he sits back even an inch, the shadow will be radically different. Then the color of his eyes startles me. I thought they were dark brown, but in this light there is a tawny copper underneath, like the bottle of marmalade which the sun strikes so it seems to pulse. He has just come from Nigeria, and how far away that is, and what he has seen. Then I realize that I have been staring with an unselfconscious intensity into a stranger's eyes. And this brother of Antoine is staring at me and we become aware of ourselves, and the intimacy is briefly but fiercely embarrassing.

He says, gesturing to the sketch book, Forgive me, it's my first time.

Weeks later in our kitchen, I say, Antoine seemed strange to me. That weekend in St. Pierre, I marked a change in him.

Late at night Maureen watched the video again and in the morning she said it was true. He had behaved differently.

I said, But he's hardly in the video at all, you can't go by that. There's a close-up of everyone playing pool. I tried to make it like John Cassavettes, swaying the camera around them, close-ups on laughing mouths, sultry eyes, chalking the pool cue. The high-pitch scrudge of chalk and cue. The camera swings around the bar and when it passes the open doorway a blast of sunshine casts a trail over the last half of the shot. A flame of blue light, an afterimage, swims briefly over the bartender and leaves a halo on Antoine's white shirt.

She's sitting on the sill of the kitchen window, a cheek and a half hefted out, so she can smoke. She turns and blows into the garden and turns back.

She says, What do you think of that? He wants to sleep with other women.

She jumps down.

Maybe I could enjoy it, she says. She holds her cigarette under the tap. I can see a tremor in her hand. Freedom, she says.

Once when we were fighting Maureen grabbed my face and kissed me on the cheek. I told her never to touch my face when I'm angry. I ran up the stairs two at a time and she was at the bottom. I leaned over the rail to shout at her. Don't touch me.

She grabbed the bannister. I'll kiss you if I want, she said. Normally, we never touch, we aren't touchy-feely.

I'll kiss you if I want, she screamed, the spitey squeak of her hand on the bannister. It was true, there wasn't a whole lot I could do about it.

She slammed the kitchen door. Then she opened it and said, I'm sorry, that was over the top.

Antoine tells me that if he kissed me it would be very different.

From what, I say.

From the way other men have kissed you all your life.

I say, Yes, I know. French kissing. We have that here, too. No big deal.

He says he isn't talking about just the tongues. He says speaking French uses a whole different set of muscles in the lips, the tongue, the mouth. A kiss is different.

But you're speaking English now, I say, you probably have your technique all fucked up.

At night he comes to Maureen with something on a fork, his hand cupped underneath. The yacht is rocking gently and the fog is already settling. He says, Ferme les yeux, ouvre la bouche.
She giggles.
What is it? she says.
You must trust me, he says.
She closes her eyes and opens her mouth. She chews once, twice. And he says, a snail.
Then she screams and spits it into her hand.

Maureen says of the woman with the blonde hair like mashed banana, A life defined solely by pleasure.
I say, Yuck.
Once Maureen held a big light for Antoine when they were trying to dock at night and he said, Get it out of my fucking eyes. It was their only fight in two months of sailing.
But he was proving himself, she says, and I could have blinded him.
She looks far away, her eyes so full of the dock and him reaching for the boat, him in the brilliant blast of light and a dark uninhabited coastline behind him.
She says, That light. And she shakes her head in amazement. Get it out of my fucking eyes, she says.
It was so heavy. It was all I could do to hold it.

After she left for France I found a diary of hers on a high cupboard shelf where we kept linen. I was alone in the house, standing on a chair gripping the dusty book. I let the diary fall open and read just one paragraph. She described a gold dress.
I snapped it shut. It was as if she were in the room, but I

could feel the longing for her too—how much I missed her. The dress was a metallic orange, shiny, form-fitting to just above the knee—and she wore it dancing. We went out and got drunk, walked home in a wind storm when the bars closed. There was a sluice of yellow leaves in the centre of Cathedral Street. We walked up the steep hill with our calves aching and the wet leaves clinging to our boots like spurs.

Michael Winter

Let's Shake Hands Like the French

I ran there in the dark and rain. I had just started running. It's a public acknowledgement of fitness. People were saying Hi Gabe, saw you running.

The rain had melted most of the snow, but there were still humps on the sidewalks from shovelled driveways. In a garden two patches of ice were melting to form a white question mark. I ran through an unfamiliar part of St. John's: Tom Brennan's Hairstylist had red and gold bars of wallpaper, a lustre of stained glass. There was a green Jesus glowing from a plexiglass booth outside St. Patrick's. The church had grey turrets that looked, in the rain, like plasticine.

I had time to admit that I was reluctant to meet Eric. This was a new year, and one resolution had been to confess to true feeling. It was exhilarating to chant aloud, as I ran, *I'd rather not see him*. By voicing it, meeting Eric became a form of choice, a willing realization that I was, if nothing else, alive. It is akin, I suspect, to a person considering his options and deciding, I'll pretend I *have* killed myself. Then you can shed obligation and unravel despair from your throat. The rest of life is a bonus, ta-da. This logic, unfortunately, is of no solace to the truly depressed. I had inherited my mother's buoyant optimism.

. . .

Eric Peach had dyed his hair black, and he hadn't forgotten his eyebrows. The fact that his eyebrows were dyed made it a more careful decision, a decision based on a mixture of craziness and vanity. He wasn't wearing glasses and there was a cigarette burn between his eyes. He wore an immense charcoal blazer. He had a big frame now.

I pointed him out to the nurse, I'm to see Eric Peach.

Gabriel English.

He liked saying my full name. It sounded respectful to him, and it honoured him that a man with such a name was coming to visit him. Or, he wanted to show that he had equivalent manners. He assumed I was a gentleman.

We shook hands and I followed him down a corridor to his room.

He said, You can spot my room from afar because the tiles change colour at the door. He said, with key in lock, The tiles anticipate the suite. He laughed and then he tried to keep the laugh to himself. I remembered then how nettled he'd get when a textbook said the paintings of Braque anticipated a such-and-such in German politics. He despised the word culmination too. Words that alluded to an insight that never existed. He hated how the idea of evolution had garnered an air of intentionality around it, as if species were thrusting themselves forwards on purpose. His mouth would turn bitter at these soft, confidently written, published sentences.

I hung my running jacket in amongst his shirts. There were no chairs so we both sat on the bed. We sat there, our feet almost touching off the edge of the bed, which made us both tight, and then he got up and lifted a pair of sneakers, a stack of CDs and two cans of Pepsi off the chest of drawers and sat on top.

I got one for you.

He handed me a Pepsi. I hadn't had a soft drink in about three years.

There was a small bloodstain on his pillow.

Two B North is the best floor in the hospital, he says. They said, Where you want to go? and I said, I want to be north. They said, Where? and I said, To be north. Two. B. North.

He had to get a light. He hid the cigarette under his sleeve. You're not supposed to smoke in the rooms, see.

He opened the door quietly, just enough to slip through.

I sat and drank the soft drink and picked up a David Bowie CD and when Eric returned with lit cigarette I nodded, wagged the CD to let him know that I remembered it, that he had given me this very album; but this fact made him stiff as it suggested how little he'd moved on since university. He had been studying piano back then, and I'd met him on the sidewalk near the laundromat shared by the residences. The left side of his moustache was stained with nicotine and a lens in his glasses was cured yellow. He had no coat even though it was near zero, and he professed to being inured to cold, that people were too obsessed with keeping warm. I sat down on the curb with him. There was a rawness coming out of his bent elbows and knees.

I've never been comfortable with material comforts. Or, I've not felt worthy of the goods and services available. Not guilty, but responsible in a vague, collective way for the massive wrongs that are done in the world to protect my standard of living. Eric was slipping off this grade and I wanted to watch him; he was my sole contact with, for lack of a better word, the oppressed. Meanwhile I shared a cement block third floor apartment with three other undergrads, where, for lunch, we split a tin of tuna (stretched into four sandwiches), and a can of condensed pea soup—young, ironic men destined to take their positions in the global frenzy of turning a buck. Our university newspaper's logo was a tender panda with FIGHT THE OP-

PRESSOR encircling it. That was me, snared by my silent acceptance of a stealthy coercion into the soup of cause and effect which explicitly governed the world's wealth, with no real feeling of remorse or sin on my part. Through no fault of my own, I would enlist into this spirit of commerce, I was agreeable, talented and a conformist. Eric: gifted, disruptive, ungrateful. He had been kicked out of university residence for setting fire to his room. His long hair had been singed by it. He said he'd placed two batteries together and then wrapped steel wool around the polarities, just like his father used to do in the woods. Flame had sputtered out and caught the curtain.

Eric spilled some Pepsi in the heel of one sneaker and tapped the ash in.

I smashed my glasses in the lockup, Gabe. I did myself some bad in there.

You look good. You look handsome.

Go way.

You do. Without the glasses. And the hair suits you. That jacket is huge.

I've got small arms, though.

He asked after Doris, was reassured when I said we were still together. Doris had always been friendly to him and I suspected he might make a play for her if ever we broke up, just because I know few people were ever kind to him. This was not anything I ever mentioned to Doris.

He had been to Toronto for eight weeks and three days. The fleshpots of Upper Canada, to use Smallwood's expression—Eric was from Gambo too, and knew all about our Father of Confederation. The best and the brightest young Newfoundlanders, laying jute-back carpet and laying nothing else, Eric said, for ten dollars an hour. He'd met a woman named Anne.

Anne with an E. He knew this because he'd asked her. She's pretty, with short hair.

I met Anne in a bar and said Can I buy you a beer? and she said No and I asked if she wanted to dance and she said No and then I met her in the cafe and, You want a coffee? She said No and I said Can I sit here? and she said I guess I can't stop you and then I asked her name and she told me and all about the E and then she left.

Then you came back.

They said I had a bomb on board. I didn't have no bomb and I was telling them that and they were getting all hysterical.

Who.

The people on board Flight 826 to Halifax and St. John's—they kept accusing me and it was ridiculous and they landed in Deer Lake, emergency landing, and I was placed into the gentle custody of our True North Strong and they drove me to the Clarenville lockup.

He tossed the cigarette in the toilet bowl and flushed it. He said, I guess you got to go now.

I asked him how long he thought he was in for. He said results of a psychiatric evaluation will take a couple of weeks and then it's up to him.

He said, Let's shake like Rimbaud and Verlaine.

And we shook hands, looking away, as we'd learned from the French.

I didn't see Eric for another three years. Every few months I'd receive a letter, usually forwarded, typed in all caps on a manual typewriter, the kind with a spool of worn, red and black ribbon, which made the letters appear half in red, as if his meaning was in flux. The letters grew shorter, and repetitive, as if he'd suddenly lost interest in the exercise and was merely keeping in touch: *Still* in Gambo, living with my parents. I drive in to Clarenville every three weeks for a lithium injection.

He'd offer a line on how hard it is to give up smoking, that he heard they add fibreglass to the tobacco. He had gone three weeks now without a beer. He listed off the new books at the Gambo library (Ayn Rand and Julian Barnes) and then, abruptly, that he should go, he supposed. His signature was large and always in the blue ink of a simple Bic. Sometimes a hasty, startling poem added to the bottom: I am dogs pounding each other dispassionately. I am dogs locked at the cock and cunt. His stamps were either the Queen or the flag, nothing fancy. Often the letters were torn down with a ruler as if he was saving paper.

Then I met him in Avondale.

This was after my brother had died and I was sometimes staying out at Helen's. I was encouraging her to take long weekends or a time out in the summer. I looked after young Martin and he educated me in the mothering of goat, chickens and rabbits. Martin knew the names of wildflowers and insects. He liked me because I resembled his father and I was noticing bits of Bruce in him. I had never thought I was much like Bruce. Martin had the English gene for long legs, but the rest of him took after Helen.

I had broken up with Doris, and split with Femke (both of whom Martin had met and liked) and begun courting Lydia. Martin was impressed with her. They had met a few times, when Lydia visited from Montreal. She was still living there and I had sent her, to this point, eighty-three letters. I was averaging a letter every thirty-six hours. Helen had warned me against infatuation. I said, how do you know you're infatuated. She said, when your work suffers.

Here I was, twenty-nine, and still unmarried. I had never lived with anyone (except roommates, for financial reasons). I didn't own a house, was still ignoring a hefty student loan, had no real job, or prospects, was not accumulating RRSPs. But I was taking care of my teeth, the fridge was stocked with my favourite foods, I went to all the movies and enjoyed buying swanky clothes and furniture second-hand. I owned a money toilet—a ten-year-old Toyota Tercel. I was living the same way I had in university and I understood this was due to my lack of commitment to the world. I couldn't buy in. I was stalled, dumbfounded by the idea of grasping an ideology. I never held an argument from a principled position the way some of my friends did. I couldn't be reliable or predictable (at least I didn't think so). Every instance seemed to be that, a particular instant, judged by its own merits, never compared. If someone said, What do you think of abortion? I said, Which abortion are you talking about? Refusing to compare meant I lacked a bank of experience to judge events by, and I knew this was a ridiculous way to run a life, but I could not abandon it for the generalizing of moments, the ranking, which was required if you adopted a philosophy. I was astonished at the depth of some people's convictions, and I confessed to undisciplined, naive views.

That's why I loved hanging out with Martin. Most children are willing to think anything, at least for a few moments. They are brimming with What-ifs. I was coldly aware, though, that in the company of Martin, I wasn't fulfilling who I was; instead I was an assistant to someone else's world, replacing his father, or Helen. I could hear a small, whiny voice: When will I be me?

I should state that there are moments I've had with Martin that have shaped me. We were fishing, once, in the pond close to Helen's house, just after Bruce had died. I was coaxing Martin's line out to a known trout, and it snapped his dry fly. At that moment a shooting star flared, banked slowly in front of us, and vanished in a sky that was more blue than black. Martin stared at me with this double luck, a moment he hasn't forgotten even though it happened half his lifetime ago.

I had the Tercel, and I would drive out to Avondale, where Helen and Martin lived. I had a desiccated gyrfalcon's claw dangling from the rear-view mirror. Martin and I discovered the claw on the stone beach, tangled in a gill net laid out to dry. The claw looked vicious in its protracted clutch. The bird had seen a fish in the net, had plunged from a thousand metres, had been caught. Years later I found out what a tercel was—a male hawk. Martin was fascinated by the claw. It dangled like some prehistoric child's mobile.

I had time to think during those drives. Sometimes I'd look at myself through Martin's eyes. He had seen me with three quite different women. I wondered what that meant to him, my instability, my uncommitted life. It seemed he easily danced from the idea of Doris, to Femke and then over to Lydia. He did not resent the loss of a person, as long as I replaced that person with someone equally nice. It was true that all three women loved Martin.

It was also true that, during these new full-blooded months of wooing Lydia, I wasn't much good to anyone. I was brooding, stunned in love, and not working. I had halted work on the novel; instead I was writing Lydia. I was thinking, even in the frenzy of my yearning, in a ruthless way: that I could use the stuff I was sending her. Cannibalize it for the novel. I kept photocopies. I was admiring the passion in my writing, but I had cultivated the professional distance to recognize that the intimacy in the passion would only be embarrassing, especially to Lydia, if made public. I'm harder to embarrass—a fact that Lydia jots down in the drawback column of going out with Gabriel English. But I knew that embarrassment was not the emotion a reader wanted to feel.

As I drove out to take care of Martin I skipped through the facts: Helen is on a week-long watercolour retreat in the Wilderness Area, with three other women in two canoes. I am to pick up Martin from the bus stop a little after three. There are notes on the kitchen table about how to take care of the animals, make sure Amanda visits, a cell phone number for Helen.

I waited in the car for the school bus. I thought, now there's something you can rely on, the shape and colour of a school bus. I watched it spit out Martin, small and seriously engaged in lugging his school bag on his shoulder.

I asked Martin what he wanted for supper and he began to censor his thought. He was a sensitive kid. He knew what was in the fridge. What was that, I said. What did you just think.

Pizza.

We drove to Sal's Pizza. We ate slices sitting on the warm hood of the Tercel. I had decided anything Martin wanted to do we'd do. I was happy here. When you have a child temporarily in your charge, life has immediate, obvious meaning. A base obligation can be a relief.

Martin was dutiful and obedient. Helen was raising him polite and mannered, which is refreshing to see in a boy. He brushed his teeth and chose two stories for me to read. He requested the bedroom door be left ajar. A wedge of hall light lay over his chest and chin. I knew how important it was not to feel cut off from the world as you're drifting asleep. The soap was wet and I knew he'd washed his face. Martin told me all the rules that had built up around him and the house. I could rely on him to be thorough with routine. We were both glad there were rules to go by.

I scanned the bookshelf and began reading a biography of Gwen John.

It was after midnight when the screen door opened without a knock. It released a hollow crack like a dropped icicle. There was a hand, then a man in the dark who looked comfortable with the porch, who knew his way around.

Oh hi. Helen here?

No.

You her husband?

For a moment I considered being her husband. I said, I'm Gabriel.

Then I could see it was Eric. And he could see it was me.

Well, well, Mr. English.

His cheekbones were swollen around the eye sockets. As if he was wearing a small pair of spectacles under the skin. His hair was cut short, in thick blunt wedges. He swung the edge of the door a little between his fingers.

I tried calling you a few times, he said, but there was no listing for a Gabriel English. Or even a G. English.

I said that I was leery of being in the book. That I didn't even have a credit card. That I used false names to order magazines, just so I'd know who *Harper's* had sold my name to.

And what do you do with that information?

I confessed I did nothing with it.

Just peace of mind, I guess, he says.

I explained I'd moved a few times, had travelled, had lost touch. Eric, gratefully, left the remainder unsaid (which was, that he'd been in Gambo the whole time and I could have reached him easily enough).

He said all last winter he shovelled Helen's driveway. He felt like Ho Chi Minh, he said. Ho had shovelled snow one winter in black Harlem.

I said that was a bizarre fact. And didn't believe him.

Again, that laugh. As if he's uncertain what he's said is funny. He touches the cold woodstove.

He said he was now a resident at Glory Path, a Home for retards, as he called it. The Home was just up from Helen's. I knew this, as there's a sign at the bottom of the road. Eric had been there about eight months.

He said, I just come over to use Helen's phone. I think I've electrified the Home.

He described how he'd been nailing up a picture in his room but it kept slipping crooked. He'd laid the picture on the bathroom floor and it slid along and slapped up against the baseboard like something out of *The Exorcist*. What, I say. What?

The nail. I think I hit some wires.

Eric Peach remains in the shadow of the porch door because the kitchen lightbulb is too strong. He is allergic to artificial light, and light reacts violently to him. He says he would appreciate my telephoning the electrician who had wired Glory Path.

Eric gives me the name—Matty Tucker—and his number. When I have Matty on I hand over the phone.

Eric relates the story to Matty. He catches my eye and points to the lamp by the phone. It had begun to flicker wildly. I turn it off. I hear him say, So, Matty, you replaced Judas? They chose you over Barsabas?

He listens to Matty's response and then hangs up. His hand still holding on to the receiver. He is a dark form quietly deciding something.

Well, Matty thinks it's just a magnetic thing. That I should go to bed out of it.

The freezer begins to click and Eric Peach says, That's giving off static electricity because of me.

The freezer emits an entirely foreign groan.

He says, I guess the youngster's in bed.
This makes me a little uncomfortable. Yes, I say.
Martin, he says. Helen gone long?
A week. She left today. (I am a man who gives out little information.)
He asks me to turn off the outside porch light and I realize he's leaving.
He excuses himself and, with each step, says Fuck. Fuck. Fuck. Back to Glory Path.
The freezer stops clicking.

I knew that Helen visited the Home, she brought goat's milk to some of the residents, as the staff calls them, and some of the residents wandered up the driveway and played with her meal rabbits. I know that Bruce tended to avoid them and, with him gone, they were coming over more often, and further up the driveway. Sometimes they sat on the old bus seat on the porch. Martin told me this.

I fall asleep jockeying through this reminder of how small life is under Newfoundland's big ear, that Eric would be here, of all places. In the morning the stairs alert me. Martin is trying to sneak up on me. The careful, slow creak indicates stealth, a trait I have. He wakes me by playing finger shadows across the sun in my face. I realize light has a weight to it, pressing on me, which his fingers relieve.

Last time I used the flat end of a nail, remember? I stroked it over your foot.
No, I say. I don't remember.
Last time when you were giving Mommy a break.
It's only 6:13 on the clock radio.
Get in, I say.
No. I'm hungry.

I ask him what he wants and he says, What is there.
There's cereal.
Pause.
I said there's cereal.
If I don't answer that means I don't want it.
There's a boiled egg.
There's toast.
There's a glass of blood.
No there's not.
Well.
An orange.

Three ginger hens have spent the night roosting in a spruce near the goat. They watch Martin as he crouches into the henhouse. With his eyes closed he feels for an egg. And out of the white hay is an egg. Voilà, he says.

Martin says the kids all sit on the bus with their knees together, lunch boxes on their laps. And they twiddle the handles, like this.

He asks if he can watch me shave.

He says, Wipe your lips now.

He sits on the toilet seat, mesmerised.

Where's the button to push down on? That's an eraser. That's what I'm calling it—it erases your skin. Wipe off your mouth now, that makes you like a clown.

He says, I used to watch Daddy shave. When he didn't have a beard.

I drive Martin down to the bus stop. The brakes are spongy and the car slides a little on the gravel. But we make the bus.

There's Amanda.

Amanda waits for him. She's a girl four years older than him. She's the daughter of the mortician and she has described to me the various stages of preparing a body. I remember being shocked that someone so young should have witnessed a vacuum sucking out bodily liquids, and chemicals injected into the head. Martin clicks out of his seat belt. Amanda stares at me through the windshield. I see her mouth ask Martin a question about me. The yellow door snapping shut and he's gone.

I make the turn gently, for the steering is shot. The deep, cold brook, and the juniper turning. I know I'm going back to bed.

I dream of Lydia. She approaches me and asks, Are you interested? And I say I am. But she is thinking I am Geoff Doyle, and Geoff appears and I have to tell her I'm not Geoff. Geoff is someone I knew in high school. He's a dispatcher now at the taxi stand on Caribou Road. Geoff has two kids and, the last time I saw him, he giggled at the astonishment of his predicament.

On Saturday we walk to the shooting star pond. I ask Martin to identify a field of dead, curled shafts. He frowns, then finds one strand that still has maroon sprigs. Fireweed, he says. In the book, he says, all the flowers are alive. They don't have pictures of them dead.

We fight in the afternoon. He wants me to call Amanda.
I'll call Amanda to the phone, but you have to ask her up.
No, you ask her.
I'm not asking her.
Ask her, he implores. Ask her ask her.
I say, Sometimes you're a pain in the arse.
He quietens, holds his breath for a moment.
I'm sorry, I say. Martin.
A huge cry blurts out. It astonishes both of us.
You hurt my feelings, he says.
I reach a hand to him.
No.

He goes upstairs. Through the banister rungs he says, I want to be depressed for ten minutes.

When Amanda speaks she leans from her chair, she makes this movement with her hands between her knees, one hand palm up, the other down with fingers clawed. She's a great story-teller.

Martin tries hard to emulate Amanda. He changes his opinion to coincide with hers. Amanda doesn't like the colour red, and Martin wavers, but decides to risk his feelings. I like red, he confesses. They sleep upstairs, at midnight, after a movie. They wanted to make a bed by me, but I said I'd sleep in the spare room.

I make pancakes for them and Amanda says, They're thin. Martin: They're flatter than a pancake. Amanda laughs at that. Flatter than a pancake, she says. That's a good one.

It's then we see Eric Peach out the living room window, leaning against the woodhorse. Amanda and Martin make googly eyes.

Eric and I follow the brook down to the road. We sit on a damp wooden bench beneath a loud willow. A fire truck screams by, slows and brakes by a house not far from the funeral home. Nothing newer than a fire truck, Eric says. He is wearing a crisp jean jacket—all his clothes seem new, or carefully laundered. I notice, in the natural light, that his face is bloated and pasty, as if he'd eaten a year's worth of deep-fried food.

We watch the polished truck reverse and manoeuvre towards a hydrant. I ask Eric about the lithium. He says it's hard to be certain, but he feels his mind is slower on it. He agrees with the doctors that it makes him reasonable. He knows his tendencies. How do I seem to you?

Frustrated, but resigned to it.

He nods a long time at this.

I felt then that I was losing Eric, like a lost packet of letters over the side of a ship. He was a man I hardly knew now, had connected to once, briefly, but now recognized him by appearance only, and even that had altered. I knew too that there was no one else like me in his world. A wind was blowing on him that had been unmolested for thousands of miles. A hot desert wind.

We notice a woman open a window in the smouldering house. She leans her fat forearms on the sill. She speaks calmly to her friend across the road, who is standing at her screen door. She smiles, as people often do in the face of personal tragedy. They are taking a heavy stretcher out of the house—they tilt the body through the porch like furniture. I see Amanda hammering a parade xylophone in her garden—silver curls around golden bars; and Martin is tossing a bicycle tire over cold telephone wires. They are both watching the spectacle. The shadow of a wire slaps black on the wire next to it. The wires moor the houses to the street. The woman's short white hands disappear as the firemen come to rescue her.

Eric rubs his forehead. He says the world must be a very dark and cold place for fire. Sometimes the heat of a memory is a forest fire in the distance. Gambo, he says, is always threatened by fire. Nothing worse than a hot wind. A fire with its light gone out. A fire with low self-esteem.

He said the day the residence was gutted he saw a woman testing a clothes iron at a yard sale. She was melting a mound of snow with it. She made a flat surface. Now why should I remember that? What's the point of that?

His hand is pressed so hard to his forehead that, when he releases, I can see the impression of eyebrows on the tips of his fingers.

We are outside the city's protection, he says. Wild dogs hunt caribou in those woods. Dogs can drag a caribou down by gripping the snout and suffocating it. This happens in Gambo, he says. All the time.

He stretches his eyes, as if through the sockets he can relieve the pressure of a massive headache. I should go, I suppose.

He clasps his knees and stands. We shake hands, looking away, but I betray our pact and watch him slope off down the road, his knees slightly bent. He has a funny gait. Amanda and Martin come running past him, and Amanda is mimicking Eric's walk now. Martin says, That's just like him. And I laugh and then feel bad.

Amanda: My Dad he don't like Eric Peach. He thinks if you hang around with simple people, you turn simple yourself.

I can see Martin agrees with this, either because he's affecting an amiable presence to win Amanda's consideration, or, through his own self-sculpting sense of right and wrong, he's judged Eric too.

Contributors

Ramona Dearing lives in Vancouver, but vows to return to St. John's soon. "Love Bites & Little Spanks" was published in Oberon's *Best Canadian Short Stories* in 1997. Another of her stories appeared in the same anthology the following year. She's also had poetry published in *The Fiddlehead*.

D.J. Eastwood, known as Jack, has published poetry, fiction and drama over the past fifteen years. Born in Alberta, he moved to Newfoundland to maintain the balance in the flow of people between the two provinces. Presently, he works at carpentry, cabinet and art making, and is slowly completing a first novel. Generally, he lives up to the "Jack-of-all" title that seems to dog his heels.

Mark Ferguson has lived in St. John's for eleven years and has been a member of The Burning Rock for over six. He is an itinerant knowledge worker. He is currently working on a long short story (amongst others) about early eighteenth-century Placentia.

Michael Jordan Jones was a filmmaker before he realized at a bus stop in Dorval, Quebec in 1996 that he was becoming a writer. He immediately went into training, quickly achieving a Proustian reclusivity. His first tale won a fiction prize in the provincial Arts and Letters Competition. "Monster Ovulation" is his first published work. He is not a Canadian writer, not yet, maybe not ever.

Jim Maunder was born in St. John's in 1959 and still lives and works there. He is a father, husband, sculptor, blacksmith, art teacher and sometime filmmaker. To relax, he likes to play with his two-year-old daughter, write stories and scripts, go out for tea and theatre, read, draw naked people, and stay up late for movies.

Lisa Moore is a graduate of the Nova Scotia College of Art and Design. She has written a collection of short stories, *Degrees of Nakedness*, published by Mercury Press, as well as art criticism and a couple of screenplays. Lisa lives in St. John's in a big yellow house that the wind blows through with her daughter and her husband, and will complete her first novel before the baby comes.

Jim Quilty has written the odd word in St. John's and Vancouver. These days he writes them in Beirut. He is from Corner Brook.

Beth Ryan is a journalist who writes fiction on the side. Two of her short stories were featured on CBC Radio's *Having Words* in 1997. She received an Honourable Mention for short fiction in the 1999 Newfoundland and Labrador Arts and Letters Competition. As a reporter, she has worked for CBC and several newspapers, including *The Globe and Mail*, *The Toronto Star*, *The Hamilton Spectator* and *The Telegram* (St. John's). These days, she lives in St. John's and teaches journalism to students across Canada through an educational project on the Internet.

Medina Stacey's fiction has been published in *Canadian Fiction Magazine*, *The Fiddlehead*, *The New Quarterly* and *TickleAce*. She recently completed "Lies Some Up and I Digress," an M. Phil thesis in three voices. She is moving from St. John's to St. Anthony, and aims to live in as many places in Newfoundland as she can, while avoiding moving to Toronto.

Claire Wilkshire lives in St. John's. Her short stories have appeared in *The Fiddlehead*, *Grain*, *Event* and *extremities: fiction from the Burning Rock*. She holds a Ph.D. from the University of British Columbia; her dissertation deals with voice and the Canadian short story. She is currently working on a collection of fiction.

Michael Winter grew up in Corner Brook, Newfoundland. His stories have appeared in many Canadian magazines and anthologies, and have been broadcast on CBC Radio's *Between the Covers*. His first book of stories, *Creaking in Their Skins*, was published in 1994 (Quarry Press). His second collection, *One Last Good Look*, appeared in 1999 (The Porcupine's Quill). Michael Winter lives in Toronto and St. John's. He is working on a fictional memoir.